FAR FROM HOME

For my parents, Robert and Thembi McLaren,
and all those fortunate enough to have experienced
a Zimbabwean childhood

JANETTA OTTER-BARRY BOOKS

First published in Great Britain in 2011 and in the USA in 2012 by
Frances Lincoln Children's Books, 74-77 White Lion Street,
London N1 9PF
www.franceslincoln.com

A catalogue record for this book is available from the British Library.

ISBN 978-1-84780-006-0

Printed and bound by CPI Group (UK) Ltd, Croydon, CR0 4YY

3 5 7 9 8 6 4 2

FAR FROM HOME

Na'ima B. Robert

F
FRANCES LINCOLN
CHILDREN'S BOOKS

A prince is a slave when far from his kingdom

Shona proverb

PART 1

Tariro

Rhodesia, 1976

They killed Farai today. Killed him and stripped him, mutilating him so that even his own father would not recognise him. Then they took him to the nearest Protected Village and forced the villagers to come and look at his broken, bleeding body.

"Look!" the white soldiers told the villagers who stood there, trying to avert their eyes, trying to block out the stench and the deafening buzz of the flies, murmuring silent prayers. "This is how the so-called 'freedom fighters' punish those who do not do as they say. And they will do this to you if you allow them to camp here, if you feed them, if you don't tell us when they are coming. We are here to

protect peace-loving people like you from these terrorists. Choose peace, not death."

It could so easily have been me. Farai and I were fighting the same war, fighting for the same dream: to take back the land. To go home again.

I miss my home, even now, years after we first left.

When I close my eyes, I can still see everything clearly, etched forever in my mind. The circular, mud house with the thatched roof where I used to sleep; the great tree in the middle of the homestead where Sekuru used to tell us stories of children taken away by witches, riding on the backs of hyenas; the fields of maize and the herds of sharp-horned cattle; the granite-topped mountains; the upside-down baobab tree; the endless sky, heavy with hopeful clouds at the start of the rainy season.

There is no time to look for rain-clouds here. There is no point. Now we live to die, not to sow seeds and help cows give birth to calves that will one day pay roora, *bride wealth, for daughters yet to come. Now my home is the bush and my family is my comrades. We, the freedom fighters.*

My bed changes every night as we follow the signs left for us by the savannah. Some days nothing happens, other days, like today, blood is spilled and my heart cannot stop flooding with terror. But I am strong, like my mother, and I cry my tears on the inside. I will mourn my brother, Farai, on the inside.

Will I ever see my home again? I do not know.

Will I ever see my father again? I do not know.

Will life ever be the same again? I do not know.

But it comforts me, comforts me and pains me, to think of how it came to this, how I came to call the bush my home.

So I will think of it now; I will remember everything that happened and try to comfort myself. And ease the pain of exile under this unfamiliar sky.

Rhodesia, 1964

1
The baobab's daughter

Many, many years ago, my forefathers came to this place, this place the whites now call Fort Victoria. They liked what they saw: the vast lands, the abundant trees, enough to build many homesteads, and the rains that came like a welcome visitor every year.

'This is a good place,' they thought. 'This is a place to put down roots.'

So they did. They cut down trees to clear the grass for fields, fields of maize and beans and peanuts, and grazing for cattle. They cut the trees into many pieces and used them to build: homes for their families, homes for their cattle, homes for their dreams of a harvest to come.

This is the land our ancestors left for us. This is how we came to call this land our home.

I am Tariro, daughter of the soil. My people are the Karanga people, our totem is *mhondoro*, the lion, and, in the year I turned fourteen, my father was the chief of our people.

My mother, Amai, loved to tell me about when I was born.

"Tariro, *mwanangu,* my child," she would begin, smiling. "I will always remember the day of your birth. It was the final days of my third pregnancy. I walked like an old woman because my joints were loose and ready for the birth. But I still went to my fields to hoe because it was planting season. All through the pregnancy, I craved the fruit of the baobab tree – those sour, powdery seeds that the elephants love so much. So I would walk to the baobab tree on the other side of the fields and, sometimes, I was fortunate enough to find that the elephants had left me some of the fruits.

"On that day I had finished my hoeing early, so I decided to go and find some of the baobab fruit. It was when I finally got to the baobab tree that the pains began. I leaned on the trunk of the tree, breathing, trying not to cry out. But the pain was so intense, I couldn't walk. I tried crawling for help, but the dry grass and stones cut my knees. I decided to go and shelter by the trunk of the tree and wait for someone to find me. But then I started to feel the baby coming, just like that! So I said to myself, MaiFarai, you will have to give birth to this baby on your own. Isn't that what our mothers used to do? And I did, Tariro. I gave birth to you all by myself, right there at the foot of the baobab tree. Your father found us there and called for the *muchingi*, the midwife. She couldn't believe it when she saw us!"

"Then what happened, Amai?" I asked.

"They took me home to my house and made me rest for many days. Your father was very worried about me. But I had never felt better! I had a daughter, a daughter I had prayed for, and I felt different somehow, changed. Giving birth to you made me know my own strength. I will always be grateful for that. My Tariro..." Then she would smile again, tears in her eyes, stroking my head.

As a baby, I spent the days on my mother's back, tied close to her, following her every movement as she pounded the dried maize to make maize-meal, the thick porridge that was my father's favourite dish. I went with her as she tended her crops, as she carried water from the river. I grew to know her smell, her voice, to know when she was happy, to sense when she was sad. Our hearts beat in time.

When at last I came down from Amai's back and began to walk, barefoot, my skinny legs poking out from under one of my brother's old shirts, I began to explore the world outside Amai's house. I spent my days wandering the homestead, playing in the grass with my brothers, looking for seed pods, discovering anthills and dung beetles, getting to know the calls of the birds. I played the games that little girls play and sang the songs that children sing.

And, while I amused myself, Amai carried another baby in her womb. After that one, Amai gave birth to four more children, my brothers and sisters. All the boys lived, but we buried the two little girls. Amai wept for her lost babies and she held me closer to her after that, fearful that she would lose me too.

I always thought that Amai had a special place in her heart, just for me. Maybe she held on to me because she never could hold those two little girls that the ancestors wanted for themselves.

2
Good news

One day, I woke to the sound of the cock crowing and Amai sweeping the dust outside the homestead. She sang as she swept, her high voice keening, rising and falling with the sweep-sweeping motion. *Shhh-shhhh, shhh-shhhh.*

"Mangwanani, Amai." I came to the door of the hut I shared with her. "Good morning, Mother."

She straightened up and smiled, her hand on her back. *"Mangwanani, mwanangu. Warara sei?* Good morning, my child, did you sleep well?"

"Ndarara, Amai, marara sei? I slept, Mother, how did you sleep?"

"Ndarara, mwanangu... I slept, my child."

Amai looked beautiful in the morning light, the small mound of her belly rising beneath her brightly coloured wrapper. Maybe it would be a girl this time.

Amai was proud of her four sons – they brought respect and prestige to Baba's family. In our language, we say '*Ane mhuri kwayo ndeane ndume, ane mhurikadzi vaeni*', which means 'One with a real family is one who has boys, one with a family of girls has strangers', as they will leave home when they marry and join their husband's clan. But I also knew that Amai secretly longed for a little girl, one of those little girls that she had lost before.

As Amai's only daughter, I had now taken more responsibility for the running of the house and caring for the children. I wanted her to get as much rest as possible, to keep her strength to nurture the baby growing inside her.

So I joined her in making our homestead ready for the day: sweeping the yard, lighting the fire, preparing the water for the porridge and for my father's bath. After that, Amai and I, along with my father's other wives and their children, went to the fields to work the land.

Harvest time was not far away. Months before, we had hitched the cattle to the plough and led them out to plough the fields in neat rows, turning the soil, getting it ready to receive the seed. Then we had planted the crops – maize, millet and *muriwo*, the leafy, green vegetable perfect for making relish.

Amai had noticed that I had a gift for growing things and she had given me a small plot of my own. There, in amongst my maize plants, I sowed groundnut seeds, knowing how much we would all enjoy the *nyimo,* gorging on slick, salty mouthfuls until our bellies ached. I also planted my favourite vegetable, pumpkin, for I delighted in its smooth, sweet taste, especially when Amai cooked it with *muriwo* and tomatoes.

Then came the time of waiting. There was little to be done in the fields until the first shoots appeared, aside from watering them. Once the plants had tasted the air, we had to look out for weeds that could easily overwhelm our crops if not dealt with swiftly enough.

For water, we younger girls, and some of the young wives too, went down to the river that meandered through the valley on the far side of the homestead. It was not a short walk but it could be shortened by the telling of a story or the singing of a song.

But the fields were always waiting, insistent, especially as the plants grew taller and showed the first signs of a harvest: hard cobs of maize, tightly wrapped in fresh, green leaves, the tassels pale and silky.

I took care of my new responsibilities joyfully, a song playing on my lips, a skip in my step, for I had a happy secret of my own: Nhamo, the only boy who could make my heart race and fireflies dance in my belly, had told his uncle that he wanted to marry me! My best friend, Rudo, who was Nhamo's cousin, told me that the family was very pleased, especially Nhamo's mother. She was Amai's good friend and I had always been careful to mind my manners when she was around, speaking respectfully, being even more helpful than usual. I wanted to make a good impression. She was, after all, the mother of the boy of my dreams.

Nhamo and I had known each other since we were children and used to swim together in the river, before we knew what shame was. He was funny and kind – and brave. He showed me how to climb to the highest caves, and once he saved me from a snake that reared up suddenly, blocking my way. Nhamo killed it with one blow from the stick he always carried with him.

"I know you are not afraid," he said, "so I will teach you how to kill them with one blow, so that they don't suffer." I knew then that I loved him, that he was like my own blood brother.

But when I began to mature, I came to understand

myself better: my feelings for Nhamo were different from those I had for my brothers. He too began to change. He became shy with me, awkward, and we drifted apart when our two worlds – the world of men and the world of women – pulled us in different directions.

At fourteen years old, I was yet light on my feet. My skin was warm and brown, like the best earth, rich and fertile. My friends all envied the gap between my front teeth, my shapely waist. I was ripe for love.

Then one day, as the sun was dipping low in the sky, on its way to the horizon, we girls were on our way back home, bringing water from the river. I balanced the clay water-pot on my head and tried to walk gracefully, head held high, back straight, as Amai had taught me. Just then, we heard the lowing of the cattle and realised that the boys were coming home from herding the cows. A rush of excitement rippled through our little group and we glanced at each other, smiles playing on our lips.

Nhamo appeared first, carrying his herding stick across his bare shoulders. He looked so strong and handsome that my heart skipped a beat. When he saw me, he stopped walking and a smile lit up his face. One of his friends nudged him and said something to the others which made them all burst out laughing.

But Nhamo didn't care. "Tariro, daughter of Makoni, you are the most beautiful girl this side of the Limpopo River!" he called out. The other girls gasped, then giggled, and I pretended not to hear, lowering my head to hide my smile, almost dropping my water-pot. Soon the cattle were lumbering past us and Nhamo was with them – but he turned to face me, walking backwards to keep up with the herd.

"I'm going to marry you one day, Tariro!" he cried.

That made the other girls start laughing out loud and they grabbed at my arms to pull me along. I laughed too and ran away with them, one hand holding the pot to steady it on my head.

But I couldn't stop thinking about him. Now sixteen years old, Nhamo was tall and broad-shouldered, with a clear brow and light, honest eyes. And fireflies danced in my belly for the very first time. That was when our separate worlds became one again.

After that fateful day when he foolishly announced that he was going to marry me, we managed to speak many times, sometimes in brief, stolen moments, more often through messages relayed by Rudo, his cousin and my best friend, and my younger brother, Tendai. The things he said to me! Enough to make me dizzy with delight. In his words, I was the sun, the moon, the stars, his very heart: *moyo wangu*. I had never felt so beautiful, so loved, so cherished. I couldn't think of anyone I wanted to marry more than him.

And then my wishes began to turn into reality. Nhamo asked me to meet him by the stream. I went with Rudo and she stayed by the riverbank, keeping watch. Nhamo's warm, brown eyes lit up when he saw me and he smiled, his hands behind his back.

We greeted each other, smiles playing at our lips, as fireflies leaped and swooped inside me.

"*Ruva rangu,*" he said softly. "My flower. I have something for you."

I raised my eyebrows, my head to one side.

"What can you have for me, *moyo wangu*?" I asked, my voice teasing.

He brought his hands out from behind his back and there, in his hands, was a beautiful orange and green striped pumpkin! I laughed with delight and clapped my hands.

"A pumpkin!" I laughed. "How did you know..?"

"You once told me that you love to eat pumpkin, and my mother decided to plant pumpkins this year.

This is the first of the harvest."

"You stole it from her garden?" I frowned.

Nhamo grinned mischievously. "No, I didn't steal it. I asked Amai for it. As a gift for her *muroora*..."

"Her *muroora*?" I exclaimed, my eyes bright. "You told her she had a daughter-in-law?" I could hardly believe it – this was my dream come true!

"Well, you know," he teased, "if this was the time of our forefathers, I could have just come to your homestead with some mice and taken you there and then..."

"Ah, Nhamo!" I giggled. "Don't tease me! You know things have changed since those days!"

Nhamo laughed. "Oh, I know times have changed! Now one needs many cattle – and money too – to pay the bride wealth. But it's all worth it... especially if the bride is as special as you. *Ruva rangu*..." My heart somersaulted as he said that. "So I told my mother about you," Nhamo went on, placing the pumpkin in my hand. "And I told my uncle – we will send the *munyai* soon with a message from our family. He will be the intermediary when we discuss the *roora*."

I laughed with joy, throwing my head back, my heart soaring. Then I looked into his warm, brown eyes. "How could your mother have ever named you Nhamo? *Nhamo* – misfortune? No, never, my love…" And we both laughed until Rudo called for me to come back home with her.

But, of course, I could not tell Baba about Nhamo. That would not have been right for a young lady, not one who was well brought-up. But I told Amai, that very night, when we were cleaning the kitchen after the evening meal.

Amai and I stepped outside the kitchen hut into the bright pool of light in the middle of the homestead. All around us, we could hear the sound of the rest of the family getting ready for bed. Children were being shushed and soft songs floated out towards us, the sounds of mothers nursing their babies, calming older children. I could see Baba sitting on his low stool with Farai, Garikai and some of the elders from neighbouring homesteads. They were taking snuff, their faces serious, their voices a low grumble.

"Amai," I whispered, touching her slim arm. "I have something to tell you." I pulled her away from the homestead, out towards the river path, the moonlight glinting silver off the mupani tree leaves.

When we had left the homestead behind us, Amai turned to me, her face full of questions.

"Yes, *mwanangu*, *chii*? What is it?"

I ducked my head and tried to hide my wide, wide smile. "Amai, it's Nhamo..." I could barely say his name.

"Nhamo?" she asked, her voice teasing. "What about Nhamo? Who is this Nhamo?" She was laughing at me, I could hear it. She knew Nhamo very well, just as she had known his mother, MaiNhamo, since before I was born. More than once the two of them had sat together in our homestead, preparing the maize for drying, or pounding the dried corn to make *upfu*, teasing me about him.

"Amai!" I whined. "You know!"

At last she became serious. "Yes, *mwanangu*, I know who Nhamo is. Did you receive some news?"

"Yes, he has told his uncle that he wants to marry me. They will soon be sending their *munyai* here to speak with Baba.... What do you think he will say? Will he accept?"

"Well, you know that depends on what his family is offering; you are the only daughter of a chief, remember that.... But I am sure it will be fine." She squeezed my hand. "The two of you do not share the same totem so there is nothing to prevent you marrying – and he is a good boy, from a good family.

I would be very proud to call him my son-in-law."

That was all I needed to hear. I laughed and hugged her tight until she protested that I was crushing the baby inside her. I quickly stepped back, but held on to her hands. I turned my face up to the night sky and felt the moonlight spilling over me, silver over silver. I had never felt so full of happiness in all my life.

The *munyai* arrived early in the morning. The sun was just creeping over the mountain when his voice cut through the crisp morning air. "*Tsvakirai kuno*! We are looking for someone to cook for us!" This was the customary call for any *munyai* hoping to speak to a girl's family about marriage.

And, as was the custom, I heard someone shout out angrily – was it my brother, Garikai? I quickly got up and ran to the door of my hut, just in time to see three men, my brother Garikai with them, armed with sticks and whips, running up the hill to where the *munyai* was standing. The *munyai* saw them coming and shouted out boldly, one more time, "*Tsvakirai kuno*!" before turning and running down the hill on the other side. The four men followed him, waving their sticks, cracking their whips.

I leaned against the door of my hut and smiled. The message had been sent. It would not be long now.

3
Homecoming

Later that morning, Baba's younger brother, Babamunini Tonderai, arrived from Salisbury. I was at his homestead with his first wife, MaiVimbai, when we heard the shouts of the children.

"*Baba*!" they shrieked. "*Baba vauya*! Father has come!"

Immediately, we heard shrill, ululating cries. MaiVimbai dropped the comb she had been holding and ran to join her co-wife and their children, who were already surrounding Babamunini. He stood broad and tall, towering over his wives and children in their bare feet, smart in his new clothes from the city. The two women clapped their hands together and laughed joyfully as he handed them bags and parcels.

"This one is for you, MaiVimbai," he said in his deep voice, his smiling teeth shining behind his moustache. "Take care, it's all the way from Salisbury! And here, MaiChipo, take this, this is your one..." MaiChipo pretended to compare her blanket with her co-wife's pot, and pouted. Babamunini looked uncertain for a moment. Then the two women burst out laughing and congratulated each other on their gifts.

"*Tatenda,* BabaVimbai," they chorused. "We thank you." Then all the children clamoured, hands outstretched. "What about me, Baba? What do you have for me? What did you bring from the city? Did you bring me a new dress? What about sweets, Baba? What about *me*?"

Babamunini roared with laughter, knelt down and swept as many of his children as he could into his arms. "Ah, is that how you greet your old father?"

I felt a familiar stab of envy. When I was younger, I used to wish Babamunini was my father instead of Baba, who never smiled, who never gave us gifts, who always walked slowly, never in a hurry, for us or anyone else. I thought it would be the best thing in the world to be Babamunini's daughter. But these were things I never spoke of, so great was my shame at my disloyal thoughts.

Chiedza, his youngest daughter, tugged his beard

and chirped, "But you aren't old, Baba! Just very big!"

And we all laughed.

Then Babamunini looked up and saw me. "*Ko,* Tariro, have you forgotten how to greet your *babamunini*?"

I dipped my knees in a curtsey and clapped my cupped hands together: "*Makadii,* Babamunini," I said, smiling shyly.

Babamunini smiled at me kindly and replied, "*Tiripo zvedu,* Tariro. I have something for you and your mother, here, wait a minute."

He reached into one of the bags at his feet and lifted out two beautiful blankets. I gasped when I saw them: they were so soft, the red colour so vibrant. A blanket of my own! Could you imagine? And me not even married yet!

I smiled broadly and dipped my knees again, taking the blankets from his outstretched hands. Amai would be so happy.

"Please send my greetings to Maiguru, Tariro," he said warmly. "I am going to greet my brother now." But this brought on a storm of protest from Babamunini's two wives and all the children. They wanted Babamunini to stay, to bathe, to eat some *sadza,* to spend time with them before going to pay his respects to my father. Babamunini considered everything, then said, "OK, perhaps I should wait until this afternoon. It will give me a chance to check on the cattle, have a look at the fields...."

They all cheered, and I said goodbye to them and set off for home.

On the way, I thought about Babamunini and Baba. Two more different brothers you could not hope to find. Where Baba was short and stout, his brother was tall and sinewy. Babamunini was full of laughter, a maker of speeches, passionate. My father was quiet, serious, avoided confrontation. It was as if the ancestors had played a joke on us, making my father the chief instead of his brother.

As it was, the spirit mediums confirmed that Baba should be chief when his father died. Babamunini concentrated on growing his family and his herd. He began to trade in the town and became very wealthy, so wealthy that he could afford to send his sons to the local mission school.

He married again and taught himself to read and speak the white man's language. But he never stayed in town for more than a week. He always said that he needed to breathe the air of our ancestors, to savour the stillness of the countryside. He was our link to the outside world. The world of the white men.

<<<<<<<<<<<<<<<<<<<<<<<

Babamunini often told us of when the white men, the *varungu,* first came to our land. He told us this story many times, as his father had told him, while we were gathered around the fire in the middle of the homestead. The flames leapt in time with his words, his evocation of our history.

"Many years ago, there was a *murungu,* a white man called Cecil John Rhodes who had made a lot of money from mining gold and diamonds in South Africa. He thought he could do the same here, on our land. He was not the only one – there were many others who thought like him: the French, the British, the Boers, the Portuguese, and they were all competing with each other for control."

"Why did they want to control us, Babamunini?"

"My children," said Babamunini, "the *varungu* were building empires, just like the Rozvi or the Zulu. But these *varungu* were greedy; greedy for our gold, our diamonds, our wildlife and our land. They wanted to use our resources to make their countries in Europe richer, to become more powerful.

"Now, Lobengula, son of Mzilikazi, king of the Ndebele, had grown concerned about all these *varungu* – the Boers, the Portuguese, the British – bothering him, wanting him to let them look for gold and other minerals in his territory. But, because he trusted the British queen's representative, he finally agreed to sign a document called the Rudd Concession, giving the British the mining rights they wanted.

But he was deceived by his advisors. They told him that no more than ten white men – ten *varungu* – would mine in the land of the Ndebele, and that they would have no guns, no weapons at all. However, they did not put that in the agreement he signed. So Lobengula did not know that the Rudd Concession gave the *varungu* the right to establish themselves and run the country as if it were their own – until it was too late."

"He signed away our country," said Farai quietly.

Babamunini nodded gravely. "Yes, *mwana wangu,* that is how the white men came to claim this land as their own: through deception and trickery. Then Queen Victoria granted Cecil John Rhodes a charter, allowing him to run the country on behalf of Britain."

"But who gave *her* the authority to decide our fate?" I asked. "We have never seen her. We did not accept her as *our* queen."

Babamunini sighed and put his hand on my shoulder. "*Mwana wangu*, Cecil John Rhodes and the others like him wanted to rule the world. Rhodes himself wanted the whole of Africa to be under British control. The truth is that the *varungu* think we are no better than animals. They think that we are savages, and that they need to civilise us. They do not even believe that the great stone city at Dzimba-dza-mabwe was built by our people! Why should it matter to them that we never agreed to obey the queen of England?"

After that, I grew sad when I thought of the history of our people. Yes, we had once defeated the Portuguese and established the Rovzi empire. We had once lived in great stone towers at Dzimba-dza-mabwe, commanded armies, controlled trade routes. But now? We were a broken people, forced to obey foreign laws, no longer free to govern ourselves.

Indeed, armed with the charter from their queen, the whites took our land and gave it away to the white settlers who came up from South Africa in the Pioneer Column. As they crossed the Limpopo River, with their wives and children, protected by their police, they named places as they went. Named them as if they owned them, as if they were the first people to call that place *home*.

It didn't matter to them that the people who lived on that land, who tilled the soil, who gave birth in the fields and buried their umbilical cords in the earth, already had names for that land. The whites liked their own names better. So when they stopped near my home, they planted a red, white and blue flag, and named the town Fort Victoria, after their queen, of course.

"The treaties, the charters, the concessions," said Babamunini, "they were meant to trick us. Our stories, our legends, our songs, have always been passed down through the generations by the spoken word, around the fire at night, just as we do now: generation to generation. We never needed to write them down – until now. Because the *varungu* are masters of the written word. They know how to make them do as they like. They use long words, careful words, tricky words. Words that can make an enemy seem like a friend. Words that can make a threat seem like a promise. Words that can make you give away your country without even knowing it."

The fire crackled as we stared into it silently, sombre, anticipating the next part of the story. Babamunini told us about Mlimo, the Ndebele spiritual leader, and how he convinced the Ndebele people to rise up against the settlers. Much blood was shed as the Ndebele tried to drive out the *varungu* from Bulawayo and the land around it. Amongst the Shona people, the great spirit mediums, Ambuya Nehanda and Sekuru Kaguvi, inspired our people to take up arms against the settlers and fight to reclaim our land and sovereignty – the first *chimurenga*, the first war for liberation.

"But we were defeated, Babamunini..."

"Yes, *mwana wangu*, the *varungu* simply had better weapons than us. They captured Ambuya Nehanda and Sekuru Kaguvi, and had them executed."

"And then what happened?"

Babamunini's face fell. "Well, the *varungu* truly established control after that. They introduced the hut tax and named the country Rhodesia..."

"After Cecil John Rhodes?"

"That's right, *mwana wangu*, after their hero... Anyway, the hut tax meant that every man had to go and earn a wage in order to pay the tax. See how sly they were? They did not need the Maxim gun after that…"

I nodded. I could see how clever the *varungu*'s plan was. I could also imagine how humiliated the men must have felt: men with numerous of heads of cattle, many wives and children, having to go and work in the white men's mines and on their farms. The dignity and honour of our men had been eroded, as surely as the Save River eats away at the riverbank.

I suppose Baba could have resisted, as Chief Makoni did in his time. He could have defied the District Commissioner. But what good would it have done? Government officials had removed chiefs from office in the past – chiefs who were 'troublesome', who would not toe the line. No, we all knew that, just as there were rewards for co-operating, there were penalties for disobedience.

Six months before, the District Commissioner, Mr Thompson, had come to visit my father with a new Deputy Commissioner, a young man by the name of Ian Watson, who had come all the way from Salisbury to 'teach Africans how to behave'.

I remember him so clearly. He was tall, much taller than any other white man I had ever seen. He was strong too, his broad back stretching the fabric of his uniform, his short khaki trousers revealing muscled thighs and bulging calves. His eye were blue, blue, his skin a fiery red, and he carried a *sjambok*, a cruel, biting whip made from hippo hide, with him always. I had seen how he shouted and snarled at the Africans who worked for him. I was afraid of him, very afraid.

Something in the pit of my stomach turned cold with dread when he looked at me with those pale blue eyes. I did not like the way his eyes swept over me, how his lips curled into a crooked smile. So I used to stay in my hut when I heard that Deputy Commissioner Watson was coming from Fort Victoria.

Very soon, I had reached our homestead and I went straight to the cooking fire where I knew Amai would be busy, preparing *sadza* for the children.

"*Masikati*, Amai," I said as I entered the hut where Amai was stirring the stiff porridge. "Good afternoon." Sweat beaded her brow and I felt instantly ashamed that I had stayed away so long at Babamunini's homestead.

"Ah, *masikati*, Tariro," she replied, with a sigh of

relief, "*waswera sei*? Did you have a good day?"

"*Ndaswera, kana maswerawo.* I did if you did." Gently, I took the wooden stirrer from her hand and she moved away from the pot, sitting down on a reed mat nearby with a quiet groan.

"*Ndaswera, mwanangu....*" Her feet were swollen and her face looked tired. "I did, my child."

"Amai," I whispered, "how did you sleep last night?"

She shook her head. "My dreams, *mwanangu*, they flew like restless birds, in and out of my mind, telling terrible stories, whispering, whispering…"

"Like the last time, Amai?" I shivered when I thought of the dreams that had plagued Amai during her last pregnancies, the ones that had ended in death.

"*Mwanangu,*" she said, a frown worrying her brow, "I feel as if something terrible is going to happen… I just don't know what…"

Just then, the hut darkened as a shape blocked the light streaming in from the doorway.

It was Baba. "*Masikati,* MaiFarai," he greeted my mother with his usual air of seriousness. "What have you prepared for us today? Did you know that my brother has arrived from Salisbury?"

Amai opened her eyes wide and shook her head.

Baba looked at me reproachfully. "Tariro," he said, "why did you not inform your mother of your babamunini's arrival?"

I looked down.

"I have told Garikai to slaughter a goat. You know how much Babamunini Tonderai loves your *sadza* with goat meat. But you must hurry, I am sure he will be hungry – you know MaiVimbai never cooks enough *sadza*! Tariro?"

"Yes, Baba?"

"Make sure you help your mother prepare the food and bathe the children."

"Yes, Baba," I replied. "Of course…"

So we did not speak again of Amai's strange dream. I helped her to cut the goat meat, still warm and oozing its living juices, before filling two pots. Then I took the children down to the river to wash – which they did while playing, splashing and screaming with delight. I, too, bathed in the shallows, enjoying the slipperiness of the cool water tingling on my hot skin. But I could not linger, even though I saw Rudo with her sisters downstream from us.

I wanted to speak to her, to tell her that the *munyai* had come, and to ask her to send a message to Nhamo.

But the children took all my time – they were like little fish, constantly disappearing below the water, only to reappear when my heart could bear it no longer. They shrieked with impudent delight when I called out to them. They knew that I was afraid of the deep, dark water. They knew that I could not come in to get them.

So I shouted at them and made them come to the river bank, threatening to beat them with Baba's cowhide whip. When they got to the shallows, I lined them all up and gave them a good scrubbing. But they could not resist splashing and teasing each other, so I slapped a few of them on the back and legs to make them stand still. Even then they were too excited: Babamunini Tonderai always brought good things from the city – and Amai was cooking goat-meat stew.

Later that night, when bellies were full and the fireflies danced in the night sky, the children sang and danced in the dust of the homestead while the elders sat around the fire, discussing the seriousness of life, taking snuff, smoking pipes. The children played *Dudu mduri,* the memory game where you name all the children of your mother and your friend's mother, in order, without stopping.

My little brother, Tendai, was always best at this game; his memory was perfect, his rhythm unshakeable.

So he called out, "*Dudu mduri*!"

The other children answered, "*Katswe*!"

Dudu mduri!

Katswe!

Farai umduri!

Katswe!

Garikai umduri!

Katswe!

Tariro umduri!

Katswe!

Tendai named all his brothers and sisters: his own mother's five children, the three from his father's second wife, the four from the third one, the one, the lonely one, from the fourth and the four from the fifth, the two sets of twins... And so the game went on, first our homestead, then the one closest to us, then another.

The game was a celebration, a celebration of childhood and of children, of lineage and heritage, of memory and rhythm. We, the older children, clapped our hands in time, laughing at the mistakes, correcting the omissions, with half an ear on the rumblings of the elders' conversation.

"It's good to be home," sighed Babamunini, rubbing his stomach, pulling on his pipe. "The ancestors are kind. My son, Kumbirai, is making good progress at school. But I fear for him. He wishes to continue with his schooling, to move to the city and find work there. But, after a while, living in the white man's city starts to destroy you. It robs you of your dignity. Just look at these passes that we have to carry, telling us where we can go, where we can work, how much we can earn!" He pulled a scruffy paper from his back pocket and thrust it forward for all to see.

The other men grumbled and shook their heads.

But Baba barely glanced at it and said smoothly, "We are pleased to hear that Kumbirai is doing so well. I am sure he will bring great honour to our family..."

Babamunini sighed. "I hope so, my brother, I hope so. It is easy to lose yourself in the white man's world, to forget where you came from, who you are." Then he shook his head, as if to clear his thoughts. "So, it will soon be time for the harvest..."

"Yes," Baba replied, "the rains have been good this year and the crops are looking healthy. It should be a good year."

"But have the authorities made any moves to claim this land? I heard rumours while I was in town..."

But Baba interrupted him. "We can speak of that tomorrow, brother. Such things are not meant for the ears of women and children. Tonight, we eat - and we drink!" And he picked up his calabash and took a long drink of our home-brewed beer, smacking his lips in appreciation. He passed it to Babamunini, who looked up and saw Farai and I standing by the fire, listening to the conversation. "So, Tariro, your father tells me that we will soon be slaughtering a cow for you, eh? Who is the lucky young man? Do I know him?"

"Babamunini, he is Nhamo, son of Macheza."

Babamunini smiled broadly. "Ah, he is a good boy, that one! I knew his father and he was a great man." He turned to Baba. "Have you had the negotiations yet?"

"No, my brother," my father replied. "You have come just in time and for that we are grateful. The *munyai* came this morning, isn't that right?"

Garikai nodded, grinning.

Babamunini laughed. "And you gave him a good beating, I hope?"

Everyone laughed and looked over at the children

who had started a new song, a song everyone remembered from their young days. And so, the talk of the elders gave way to the song of the children who danced, stamping, twirling, arms in the air, golden in the flickering firelight.

4
News

The next day, we all slept later than usual. The heat of the morning had risen and I woke up hot and damp, my mouth parched. My dreams had been very vivid: I was looking for Nhamo in a burning field, and I could hear the sound of angry men's voices. Then I saw him walking ahead of me and I ran after him, the earth around me black and smoking, but I could not catch up with him. The smoke began to sting my eyes and I couldn't see any more and when I woke up, my eyes were sticky with unshed tears.

I sat up slowly and held my head in my hands. What had the dream meant? Unlike Amai, I never dreamed in prophecies, seeing the shape of things to come. My dreams were always simple, forgettable, and I hardly ever thought about them in daylight. But that morning, I could still smell the acrid smoke, the prickle of burnt grass under my feet, the black soot coating my legs. And my voice, as I called Nhamo to wait, wait, wait for me. He had not looked back, walking on until he disappeared from view, leaving me rubbing my eyes with soot-covered hands, making black marks on my face.

I reached over and soothed my burning throat with water from a calabash. I could hear Amai sweeping outside, so I washed my face and quickly went out to greet her, remembering for the first time that we had not spoken about *her* dream.

But, as I rushed outside, I heard the sound of a bicycle bell and rubber tyres, soft on the fine dust of the footpath. Amai heard it too and straightened up, her hand on her back, one hand shading her eyes from the mid-morning sun that played in the dust.

It was a messenger from Fort Victoria. "*Mukai, mukai*!" he shouted, his voice scarring the sleeping silence of the homestead. "Wake up, wake up!"

Amai glared at him. "Is this any way to greet people?" She clicked her teeth. "Some people have forgotten everything their parents taught them!"

The young man was suddenly ashamed. He lowered his head and said, humbly, "Please forgive me, Amai, I forgot myself. I have a message for the chief from the District Commissioner."

Amai motioned to me and I went to fetch my father, who was sleeping at MaiZiyanai's house. Standing outside at a respectful distance, I called to him.

"Baba! There is a man here to see you. He says he has a message from Fort Victoria."

Baba emerged, tucking his waist wrapper round his middle. He nodded his thanks and walked slowly to where the young man was waiting, in the middle of the clearing.

The man seemed to have remembered his manners and clapped his hands respectfully, greeting Baba formally as was our custom. "The District Commissioner says that you are to assemble the members of the *dare* council here this afternoon. He has very important news and he does not want to have to go to each homestead one by one. So you must all come here and he will speak to you all."

My father looked offended. "What is it he wants to talk about? Can he not speak to me in private? I am, after all, the leader of my people. If he has anything to tell them, he can tell them through me."

The messenger looked embarrassed. "Actually," he confided, "it was the Deputy Commissioner who insisted that he speak to all of you. Baas Thompson wanted to discuss with you privately but Baas Watson said, no, these native chiefs must not get too big for their boots. He wants to speak to the people direct."

"So, Watson is coming, not Thompson?"

The messenger nodded.

I felt a sense of foreboding when I heard this. I could not understand why.

I could see that Baba was not pleased, as he pressed his lips together and clenched his fists round his walking stick. But what could he do?

"Tell him they will be here," Baba said at last, and his shoulders sagged, just a little.

The messenger thanked him gratefully and ran back to pick up his bicycle.

Baba turned and looked at us, and the other wives and children who had assembled. "We should prepare ourselves for bad news," he said shortly, and turned to MaiZiyanai, suddenly irritated. "What are you waiting for, woman?" he barked. "Prepare my tea and my bath!" And he stalked off, to brood over the meeting to come.

That afternoon, the men began arriving from the surrounding homesteads. My brothers had all been sent to call the men of the other households, to summon them to the meeting with Deputy District Commissioner Watson. So they came, feet dusty, beads and snuff bags slung over their shoulders, shiny, worn jackets that were too small or too old to be worn by their sons in town, dusty overalls hanging from the bony shoulders of old men with grizzled beards.

They all sat in a circle, some lost in their own thoughts, others talking with their friends in low voices, all of them waiting, waiting. My heart skipped a beat when I saw Babamunini sitting with Farai and Nhamo. But they were deep in conversation and I could not catch Nhamo's eye.

We, the women of the chief's family, waited inside, hoping to hear the news from Fort Victoria. The heat of the morning had ripened and swelled in the homestead, stifling the breeze, the air thick and heavy with the smell of wood smoke and wild flowers.

Then they came, Deputy District Commissioner Ian Watson and his Africans from Fort Victoria. The younger children stared open-mouthed at the glinting steel of the guns the men carried, at the hardness in their faces. These were not our uncles, these men, though their skin was like ours. They were from the west of the country and they spoke Ndebele, rather than Karanga. It was a favourite tactic of the white man: to divide and rule. In our case, they had succeeded, for we knew from bitter experience that the guns they carried were not just for show.

In the middle of the group of men came Deputy Commissioner Watson, his blue eyes cold, his hands behind his back, holding his *sjambok*. He nodded at my father, who came forward to greet him. But Watson simply stared at Baba's outstretched hand, then looked away.

I understood immediately. Watson was one of those *varungu* who did not touch Africans. Everything about him – his imperious stare, the straightness of his back, the way he carried his head – spoke of arrogance and entitlement, and my nerves bristled to see my father snubbed by someone less than half his age.

Then Watson cleared his throat and spoke, his voice clear and formal, as if he was making a speech he had rehearsed. "It is my duty to inform you that, as you already know, a law was passed by the government in Salisbury in 1951. That law was the Native Land Husbandry Act and, until now, the government has been slow to implement it. All that has changed, thanks to more dedicated administrators becoming involved." He looked around at us all and smiled briefly. "Now, you all know that the government in Rhodesia has tried to treat you people fairly and has looked after you. In fact, the Native Land Husbandry Act is yet another way of the government showing how much it cares for you Africans. This law will allow you to learn how to farm properly, instead of keeping too many cattle, cutting down all the trees and allowing the soil to become eroded. The white men who will be given this land you are on now will work for the good of the country: they will plant tobacco and cotton – cash crops – and they will keep cattle for export..." He stopped and looked around at the blank faces of our elders, who did not speak English, and his lip curled.

His African assistant turned to him. "Should I translate, sir?"

"Ag, don't bother, Petros!" Watson sneered. "What's the point? They won't understand, no matter how much you try and explain. These people haven't got a bloody clue – can't you see from their faces? Just tell them that they've got two weeks to get their things together – the trucks will be here to move them to the Native Reserve. They'll soon learn that there is more to life than dancing and drinking beer, eh?" He chuckled and Petros laughed with him, showing all his teeth.

Petros then turned to face the men, who had been following his exchange with Watson, and with exaggerated formality he began to give a speech of his own. "Baas Watson came here today to tell you that this land is going to be reallocated, according to the Native Land Husbandry Act of 1951. You have two weeks to arrange your affairs before the trucks come to take you and your families to your new homes."

Baba simply stared at Petros, disbelieving, but Babamunini and the other elders were not so calm. Several of them began to shout out in protest, waving their sticks at Petros, spitting on the ground. Amai and I exchanged glances. What was going to happen?

"New home?" Babamunini barked, his brow creased, his eyes angry. "What do you mean 'new home'? This is our land and the land of our forefathers! This is where our ancestors are buried, where we have sown our seeds, where we raise our children. This is our home – and it has always been!"

Another elder spat in the dust and glared at Petros. "We will not let our land be taken from us! How dare you come here with such abominable speech?"

The other men all nodded in agreement.

An older man, his mouth showing more gaps than teeth, struck the ground with his walking stick and said, "How can they tell us to leave our own land? Do the spirits not expect us to honour them here? If we leave, who will perform the rituals to honour the dead? No! To abandon our ancestral lands would be to invite the wrath of the ancestors upon us!"

Petros dropped his official demeanor and looked contemptuously at the old man. "Do you really think that your talk of spirits and ancestors will change the white man's mind? Look, you are on good land here and the *varungu* want it for their farms, to grow cash crops like tobacco and cotton..." The men's voices rose again, almost drowning Petros's voice but he continued, ignoring them. "And they have prepared another place for you to live, just south of here. You have two weeks to pack up and leave."

This resulted in a frenzy of shouts, accusations, choked insults and curses. At the sound of the suddenly raised voices, the African messengers from Fort Victoria looked at each other fearfully, unsure what to do. They had seen that several of the men carried deadly knobkerries, while others held their walking sticks in both hands. I saw the glint of a *panga* blade.

Watson frowned and shouted at Petros. "Hey, keep these natives under control, man!"

But it was too late. The group of men seethed as one body, arms raised, fists clenched, ready to vent their anger on the colonial servants.

The homestead echoed with raised voices, and scuffling feet churned the dust. For a moment, it looked as if the men were going to take every single messenger and beat him senseless.

Out of the corner of my eye, I saw Babamunini and Nhamo start towards DC Watson. He saw them coming and, with a curl of his lip, he reached down and drew out his gun.

5
Confrontation

Deputy Commissioner Watson fired his gun into the air, once, twice, then pointed it at Babamunini. Immediately the men fell back and the messengers, panting with fear, sweating, managed to free themselves and reach for their own weapons. The metal of their guns glinted in the sunlight as they pointed them at my father, my uncle, my brothers, my beloved Nhamo.

Petros, coughing and spluttering, struggled to retain his dignity.

Watson gave him a hard look and barked, "That's why you'll never get that promotion, Petros. You can't even control your own people! You're useless, man, pathetic!"

Petros turned to glare at the villagers. "You are all mad if you think you will get away with this! I am a representative of the Queen of England!

And I *will* be respected!"

But Babamunini would not back down. Breathless, his chest glistening with sweat, he snarled, "You are nothing but a sell-out! A despised servant who cannot even share a cup with the white *baas* you love so much!"

Petros shot him a dark look and then turned to Baba,drawing himself up. "May I remind you that you are a servant of Her Majesty, the Queen of England, and that, by law, you must obey our orders?" His voice took a vicious turn. "And remember, the only reason that you are still the chief is that your grandfather made the wise decision to comply with the *varungu*. Otherwise, you would have found yourself with nothing: no wives, no children, and no land. Not even a *badza* to call your own. Remember that! You owe your allegiance to the queen in England now, the one who pays for your snuff."

All eyes were on Baba, waiting for him to assert his authority, to tell this bush-pig to go back to his mother's womb. But Baba just stood there, clenching and unclenching his fists, and the moment passed.

A movement rippled through the group of men: a slumping of shoulders, a heaving of chests, a shaking of heads. And a new look of disdain flooded their eyes when they looked at Baba, as emasculated as a castrated bull. The defiant, aggressive atmosphere dissipated as my father withstood the disappointed looks of the people he was meant to lead.

Petros savoured the moment, and then turned away scornfully. "You may go, all of you!" he called out. "And remember, two weeks and the trucks will be here to take you to your new home."

The men filed away, murmuring, casting sidelong glances at Baba as they left. Soon, the clearing was almost empty. Only Baba, Babamunini, my brothers and Nhamo remained, as Watson, Petros and the others prepared to leave.

Watson, putting away his revolver, turned to Petros and said, "Hey, Petros, remember what I told you back in Fort Vic? I want a girl to come and work for me at my house…"

Just then, my youngest brother ran out into the clearing. I hissed for him to come back but he ignored me. I had no choice but to come out of Amai's house and go after him. I felt all eyes on me as I scooped him up into my arms.

Then I saw Petros grin and point towards me. "What about her, baas? Would you like her? She's pretty, eh?"

Watson turned his head, then walked back to get a better look. His eyes swept over me, from my braided hair to my bare feet. Then he smiled, a smile that reminded me of the crocodiles that wait for their prey on the riverbank, waiting, half-asleep, until a mother turns her back. It made the blood rush to my face.

And then, to make it worse, he actually spoke to me. "Come here, girl," he called, beckoning me.

I faltered and looked at Baba. Did I really have to do what this white man said? Baba nodded his head stiffly, and his eyelids flickered. He put out his hand and I walked to where he was standing. Protectively, he put his hand lightly on my shoulder. But now Watson was loping towards me, his eyes never leaving my face. Baba drew me closer to him as Watson approached but, without so much as looking at my father, Watson simply tapped him lightly on the chest with his *sjambok* – a silent command to stand back.

Baba had no choice but to obey and leave me, his only daughter, standing in the middle of his homestead, being looked over by a white *baas* from Fort Victoria.

Watson stood close to me, so close that I could smell him: sweat, leather and ironed cotton. I could see the pale hairs on his forearms, the cut on his left knee. Arms, knees, legs; this was all I saw because my head was bowed low with shame. He walked slowly round me, his eyes burning trails all over my body. He felt my upper arm for muscles. He slapped my right thigh with his *sjambok*. Inside, I was screaming. My heart rebelled against the indignity of being poked and prodded, like a cow that was about to be sold.

And so, even though my face burned with shame and tears stung my eyes, I forced myself to look up, to look my tormentor in the face, to look into his blue, blue eyes with my blazing brown ones. I caught his eye as he stopped in front of me. He was so close that I could smell the tobacco on his breath. There was a moment of surprise that I dared to look him in the eyes, then the hint of a smile. A cruel, sadistic smile.

"I see we have a feisty one here, Petros," he laughed, casting a glance over his shoulder. "But do you think she's feistier than my horse, Milly?"

And, with that, he grabbed hold of my lower jaw and pulled my mouth open, pushing his grimy thumb between my teeth, feeling my molars.

I could taste him. My stomach lurched and I gagged, tears stinging my eyes.

I did not think.

I bit down. Hard.

Watson let out a cry of pain and surprise and brought his other hand, balled into a fist, crashing into the side of my face. The pain exploded, red-hot and furious across my cheek, and I let go of his thumb and fell to the ground, gagging and retching. That was when Amai appeared. She flew to me, screaming, holding her protruding belly, and put her arms around me as I lay there in the dirt.

Just then, there was a strangled cry and Nhamo, all glowing skin, taut muscle and eyes spitting fire, leapt forward and slammed into Watson, knocking him off his feet. In seconds, he was straddling him in the dust, shouting curses, his huge fist exploding in Watson's face. Blood spurted from Watson's nose and soon Nhamo's hands were slippery with it.

It took a few moments for Watson's men to realise what was happening and react. Some of them held their weapons up at Babamunini and my father, while two of them tried to haul Nhamo off Watson, who writhed, bleeding, on the floor of our homestead.

But two men were not enough. After all, this was Nhamo, the boy who had defeated a lion single-handed. Soon, five of them were struggling to hold Nhamo so that Watson could get up, staggering and holding his nose. I recoiled at the sight of him. His face was covered in blood and his blue, blue eyes glittered with rage as he pointed at Nhamo.

"You'll regret this, you bloody *kaffir*!" he screamed, his voice twisted with pain and fury. "You dare to touch me? You dare to touch me?" And, forgetting about his own broken nose, he drew his fist back and swung it at Nhamo's face.

We heard the crack. We saw the blood. I watched as Nhamo struggled to free his arms, fought to protect his head, tried to duck the blows. But it was no good. All we could do was stand and watch while Watson punched Nhamo again and again, all the while calling him a *filthy munt* and a *dirty kaffir*. We could do nothing because the guns were ready now, the sticks raised. I had to cover my mouth to keep from crying out.

When Watson was done, he hauled himself away, panting, holding a handkerchief to his nose. Sweat was running down his face, mingling with his blood. He made a motion with his hands and, in a flash, Petros and the other Africans fell on Nhamo with their *sjamboks*, those whips that draw blood on first contact. Blood spurted like flame lilies from Nhamo's back as the men turned him over and whipped him again and again and again.

It was Petros who began the kicking. First his back, then his belly and then his head, as Nhamo tried to curl his body, as in his mother's womb, to protect himself from their blows. Watson mopped his forehead and licked his bleeding lips as he watched, a look of satisfaction on his face.

Seeing my beloved like that, so helpless, I could not hold myself and I sprang forward and tried to pull one of the men off him but he knocked me down with one sweep of his arm.

Eventually Watson called the men off. They gave Nhamo one last kick and then hauled him up to drag him to the waiting vehicle.

I scrambled to my feet and ran towards them. "Where are you taking him?" I screamed at them.

The guns turned on me immediately but, although I felt a cold wave of dread wash over me, my blood was too hot. I pushed them aside and ran to Nhamo. His eyes were swollen shut, his face a mess of crimson blood and purple bruises.

"Nhamo, Nhamo," I moaned. "What have they done to you, *moyo wangu*?"

Watson swung himself up into his truck and glared at the terrified huddle of men, women and children who had, by now, gathered in the homestead to witness the scene. He waved his gun over their heads. "Let this be a warning to you all!" he shouted. "Don't get any silly ideas in your heads. You have two weeks to get your things and move to the reserve. My men will be here to make sure that everything goes smoothly."

"But where are you taking him?" I screamed again, hot tears searing my cheeks, my face contorted with anguish.

"As for this one, don't you worry about him," muttered Watson grimly. "He has assaulted one of Her Majesty's officers. We'll teach him a lesson he'll never forget..." Then he turned the key and the engine roared. "Come on, you boys, *checha,* hurry up!"

And they left, carrying my brave, foolish, bleeding Nhamo with them.

When they had gone, all that could be heard was the worried murmuring of the men, women and children and the high, keening cry that came from my throat as I sank to the ground and sat rocking, my hands pressed to the red soil where Nhamo's blood bloomed in dark patches. I felt as if my heart had been torn in two.

I could not look in Baba's eyes that night.

6

Meeting of elders

I couldn't sleep after they took Nhamo. My dreams were haunted by visions of his battered and bleeding face, the thick sound of Petros' boots in his side, the sickening whistle of the *sjamboks* as they sliced the air and cut my beloved's flesh to ribbons. And I knew I was to blame! I should have stood still, I should not have provoked Watson. But what else could I have done? Later I shed many tears over the choice I made – and its terrible consequences.

Amai had been badly affected. I made her sleep while I cooked the *sadza*. I took the children to play by the river, to let her rest.

"Tariro, no," she insisted weakly, "let them stay here…"

"Amai!" I cried. "Think of the baby! You must rest … please…"

As for me, I shed tears every night, trying to bury

my sobs in my new blanket so that Amai and the other children wouldn't hear.

I could see that Baba was worried about Amai but, every time he came into her hut to ask her how she was feeling, she turned her face away and cried silent tears to the wall. When Baba looked over at me, I lowered my eyes so that he would not see them accusing him, full of reproach. *You stood by and let them do that to Nhamo. How could you? What kind of chief are you? What kind of man are you?*

Silent questions, never to be uttered.

In the end, he turned away from my mother's back and sent for *Ambuya*, my grandmother. "It must be the pregnancy," I heard him mutter as he walked away to the meeting that the elders were holding to discuss the latest news from Salisbury, to decide how to move the families, cattle and our belongings.

<<<<<<<<<<<<<<<<<<<<

Farai was at the *dare*, the meeting held between my father and the other men of the village, and he told me later what happened.

"There were many of us, Tariro," he said breathlessly. "Everyone wanted to talk at once, everyone had something to say. Even some of our men who work in the city came back home to discuss the latest news, to decide what to do. Babamunini was there, but he was not sitting next to Baba as is customary. He was seated a little away from the group, watching everything.

"Baba spoke first and said, 'We must now decide how to move our families to the new homesteads. We are many and it will take some planning and hard work to make sure we are ready to leave by the time the white men come back again.' His voice was flat, showing no emotion."

Sounds like Baba, I thought to myself. "Go on, Farai," I urged him, "tell me what happened."

"Some of the elders started talking about the reserve, where it was, how long it would take to get there, the impossibility of bringing in the harvest before the deadline. Babamunini, the men from the city and we younger men all watched them, saying nothing. I could see from the way Babamunini was clenching his fists – you know how he does it just like Baba – and the way the muscles twitched on his back, that he was getting angrier and angrier. At last, he could keep quiet no longer. He stood up abruptly – you know how tall he is – and everyone fell silent. He looked at us, every one of us, his eyes cold with disdain.

"'So,' he sneered, 'we have come together to talk, not about action, not about resistance, or even negotiation, but about how we are going to surrender our land, the land of our forefathers. No mention whatsoever of the disgraceful way we were treated by that deputy commissioner. No mention of his atrocious behaviour. No word about how one of our young men, one of our finest young men, now faces prison and worse for defending the honour of one of our daughters?' He glared around at all of us and I felt the hairs on the back of my neck rise as his eyes met mine – for Nhamo did what I should have done.

"One of the young men who had been sent to the mission school and had left the village last year to work on the railroads stood up and said, 'It's true. What you all saw was only a taste of what these whites are capable of. Those of us who work in town, we know these whites better than you. They will not let that young man get away with defying them. They will make an example of him.'

"Then Baba said, 'Brother, the reason I do not speak of the events of this week is that they have passed now. I have already arranged to go and speak to District Commissioner Thompson about the affair. I am sure he will listen to me. He is a good man…'

"'The whites are all the same, brother,' said Babamunini gravely. 'They all see us as inferior. They are all colonialists… it's just that some are less harsh than others.'

"But Baba protested, 'Now you are being unfair. What about the missionaries? Those who educate our children and provide medicines…'

"One of the older men stood up shakily and faced the group. 'Were we without medicines before the whites came? Did we not have herbalists who knew which plants could be used to cool a fever, or stop a runny stomach? And did the whites not bring their diseases with them? And their education – what does it serve but to alienate our children from our language, our customs and traditions?'

"The railway worker added, 'And after all that education, we are still only fit to serve the whites tea and call them *baas*!'

"Babamunini leaned forward. 'Know this: the whites will never allow us to run our own affairs. How can we, when even our own chiefs owe their allegiance to the queen? And those who try to resist and assert their independence are quickly replaced –

or silenced in other ways.'

"'You must realise,' added the railway worker, who really seemed to know a lot about the whites and their ways, 'that this new law is specifically meant to undermine the chief's authority – from now on, it will be the government that allocates land, not the chief, as it has always been. Some people will own their land themselves, unlike our way of sharing the land communally, giving to whoever needs it. This system is what allows those of us who work in the city to maintain our homesteads in the communal areas and come home whenever we want to take a break or till the soil or help with the harvest.

"Under the new law, this will no longer be possible. We will be obliged to farm full-time or work permanently in town or on white-owned farms, in order to be able to pay taxes and buy goods for our families.' He adjusted his spectacles. 'This is their aim, my brothers: to divorce us from the land and make us dependent on earning a wage so that we will always be under them.'

"Babamunini nodded. 'What you have said is true, young man. When a man farms the land of his forefathers, he is like a king, with roots and dignity. Once this is taken from him, he becomes nothing more than a peasant – or a beggar. It is clear that we will not be able to win the white man's game if we play by his rules.'

"The young men nodded and growled their agreement. I saw Baba look down. I felt bad for him then.

"Babamunini turned to our father. 'Son of my mother, you are our chief and, by law and custom, the decision is yours to make. But, if we let them move us out of here, when will it end? When they have finally taken all the good land for themselves? We have heard tales about these so-called *native reserves*. They are barren wastelands where crops struggle to grow a little before they die because there is no rain; where the cattle's skin stretches against their ribs, their milk thin and watery because they are overcrowded and the land is overgrazed. And they want to herd us together to live in these graveyards, to be watched by their spies, to be controlled by their commissioners. And surely we will see our children's bellies grow round with disease and malnourishment; we will see our wives old before their time, dropping their babies too early, our manhood wasting away. And then, when hunger has us by the neck, when the life is being squeezed out of us, they will come with their generous offers – to be their workers, their servants, their garden boys, to earn money to feed our families. To feed our families! The very families they starved!' Babamunini laughed then, a harsh, grating, bitter laugh. 'No, no, my brother,' he said in a low voice, shaking his head. 'We cannot allow this to happen. We *have* to fight – we have no choice!'

" Several of the young men cried out in agreement but our father shook his head. 'Fight, my brother?' he said quietly. 'How can we fight? Where is your army? Where are your weapons? What use are your loud cries against their guns?'

"Several of the older men nodded their heads in agreement. Our uncle looked at Baba then, in a way I had never seen him look, and a chill ran through me. 'My brother, I would rather face those guns and lose my life fighting, than put my tail between my legs and slink away to live a quiet life of shame.'

"And he turned and stalked away, leaving a shocked silence behind him. Then Baba looked at us all and said stiffly, 'No matter what, I am still the chief, and I will make the final decision, regardless of what those who are young and hot-headed have to say.'

"None of us could look Baba in the eye after that, and the meeting was brought to an end."

"*Ndatenda*, Farai," I cried, my voice catching. "Thank you for coming to tell me." Then I heard Amai call my name. I bit my lip and tears stung my eyes. "And you… you said Baba was going to ask about Nhamo?"

"Yes, that is what he said," Farai replied. "He will leave with Nhamo's uncle in the morning."

"Do they know what will happen to him?"

"Could be a prison sentence… attacking a government official, a white one especially, is a very serious crime. But Baba said he would talk to Thompson, so let's hope…"

Tears sprang to my eyes and Farai stroked my cheek. "You must be strong, Tariro," he murmured. "We must all be strong." Then he got up. "I must go now."

"Where are you going?" I asked.

Farai avoided my gaze. "Some of the other young men want to talk to Babamunini and the railway worker – he thinks there may be a way to resist going to the reserve."

My eyes opened wide with fear. "Farai," I breathed. "Please don't go against our father. He is the chief – we must await his decision…"

Farai gave me a hard look then. "My sister,"

he said icily, "our father should have thought of that when he allowed himself to be humiliated in front of the whole clan. The time for weakness is at an end. And those who cannot see that will be swept aside."

I swallowed thickly. "What are you saying, Farai?" I grabbed his arm and hissed at him. "What are you *saying*?"

"It doesn't concern you," he replied shortly, pulling his arm away. "I have said too much already. I must go." Then he smiled at me. "Wish me well?"

"*Famba zvakanaka*," I said, blinking back tears. "Go well."

And then he was gone, disappearing among the mupani trees as the sun began to set, staining the sky as red as blood.

7
Lions begin to roar

The next few days were unbearable for me. I hated the tension in the house – Amai's silent, pent-up anger, Baba's wounded pride, Farai's barely concealed contempt for Baba. Baba had announced that we would follow the District Commissioner's orders to leave and he ordered us to begin preparing our belongings. He was increasingly isolated as the others chafed against his decision.

Many times I saw him sitting alone, lost in his thoughts, morose. Farai and Garikai hardly ever sat with him now. Babamunini stopped coming. Farai took to staying out with Babamunini, returning so late that the fire had long gone cold by the time he lay down with the other boys. I knew this because my youngest brother, Tendai, told me. Of course, I knew little of what went on with the boys on their side of the homestead; I had worked, played and slept separately from my brothers since before becoming a woman.

I knew even less about what Babamunini, Farai and the other young men discussed when they went to the other homesteads – but I had my suspicions. I couldn't stop thinking about what Farai had told me. Surely they didn't think they could resist the orders of the *varungu*? And what if they did? What would Baba say? And what would he do to Farai if he found out that he was planning to disobey him? This was more than disobedience – this was a betrayal of the worst kind.

Finally, I could bear it no longer. I waited for Farai at the edge of the maize field just before sunset, when I knew he would be coming home with the cattle. Farai's face broke into a smile when he saw me and he whistled and clicked his teeth at the cows, motioning for the younger boys to continue with the herd without him.

"Don't forget to fasten the gate!" he called after them. "There are thieves around these days and I heard lions last night. They sounded close, so take care."

"I heard them too," I murmured, remembering the chill that had slipped through me, an icy trickle down my back, when I heard the lions' roars floating on the night air. But, unlike Farai, my first thought had not been Baba's cows – it had been Nhamo.

Tears had pricked my eyes as I thought of the scar that he bore from his fight with a lion – and I remembered again the terrible sight of his broken, bleeding face and felt again the gnawing pangs of guilt. If it hadn't been for me and my rash actions, Nhamo would never have attacked that jackal, Watson. And he would be here now, with us.

Oh, Nhamo, Nhamo. How many scars do you have now?

"You heard the lions too, sister?" Farai turned towards me.

"Yes," I replied. "They sounded like a group of about five or six, a few cubs with them, to the east of here."

Farai smiled. "You were always good at understanding the sounds of the bush..."

"Not any more," I said. "Now I hear footsteps in the night, and I don't know where they lead. I hear whispers in the dark and I do not know what they say. I feel change on the wind but my heart is unsettled."

Farai looked at me intently and I could see that he had understood my meaning. "Change must come, sister," he said softly. "That is the way of the world. And sometimes, tears must be shed for the change to occur. Indeed, sometimes, life must be lost for new life to begin."

But tears filled my eyes then. "No more riddles, brother!" I cried. "Please, tell me the truth: what is happening? Where do you go every night? Why are you not helping us prepare to leave? What are you planning? Does Baba know?"

Farai put his finger to my lips and shook his head. "Too many questions, sister. These things are not for you to worry about. These are the concerns of men – you should not lose sleep over them..."

"What?" I cried. "How can you say that? Don't the actions of you men, your choices, affect us all? Do we not carry the burden of your decisions? Do we not suffer the pain and humiliation when you give up? Do we not bury the dead when you decide to stay and fight?" Then I looked at him hard. "Do you think that because we tend the fields and carry babies on our backs that we do not have eyes to see? That because we spend our days cooking and washing clothes in the river, we do not understand the words that are said when you men are *padare*, in council?"

"*Aiwa*, sister, no. That is not what I am saying.

It's just that..."

"Then tell me what is going on! I have a right to know! I have a right to know whether I will be saying goodbye to my home... or saying goodbye to my brother..."

Farai nodded gravely then looked round before taking me by the arm and leading me into the bushes. "Tariro," he said, his voice low and stern, "I am trusting you..."

"You know you can trust me, brother."

We walked together in silence until we reached a small hill, crowned by granite rocks. Farai took my hand and, just as we had done as children, we began to climb the hill together, our feet finding the familiar footpath hidden by the wild grass. Once we reached the top, we found a smooth rock to sit on. It was still warm from the afternoon sun that was shimmering, orange, just above the horizon. From there, we could see our homestead, the cattle enclosure, the fields that surrounded it, swaying green with maize soon to be harvested, the stream that provided water for the family and ran right down to join the great river beyond the hills. Further away, beyond the sea of msasa trees, I could see the baobab tree – my baobab tree – and, in the distance, I could just make out the ruins of the ancient city of Dzimba-dza-mabwe.

As the last breath of daylight stroked my face, my heart swelled with love, a warm, sweet love, for this beautiful land, for my home - and for my brother. I turned to him and saw him gazing down at our home, fire in his eyes.

He turned to me. "Do you see what I see, sister?"

"What do you see, brother?"

"This is *our* land, Tariro," he said fiercely, "*our* land. The land of our ancestors. We will not leave, not without a fight."

"But Farai," I said gently, "What about Baba? And the elders? They have already decided…"

"Don't talk to me about them!" he spat out, and I recoiled at the scorn in his voice. "I would rather die than allow the whites to take away all that I have, all that we have… this land is our birthright, Tariro. Without it, we are nothing…"

"But Farai," I protested, "Baba is the chief! And he is good to us, a good father, a kind man…" My voice trailed away when I saw the hard look in Farai's eyes.

"*Moyovochena unobayisa,*" he said, stabbing his finger in the air. "A kind heart gets one killed. Baba's back is bent from bowing to these whites all his life,

Tariro. He has allowed them to strip him of his power, his authority and his dignity. At the end of the day, an elephant is not burdened by its own tusks – you have to stand up for your responsibilities." He took a deep breath. "Our father is no longer fit to lead our people."

My heart skipped a beat and I stared at him, too shocked to speak.

He glanced at me and turned away. "Don't look at me like that, sister. You know it's true."

And, in spite of my love for my father and my inborn, ingrained respect for him, I knew that Farai was only saying what I had known for some time, what Amai felt, what others could see. But to have the audacity – the folly – to say such a thing out loud? This was a step too far. For when a son can tell his father that he is naked, disaster is sure to follow.

"Tariro," Farai interrupted my thoughts, "we *will* fight the whites when they come. Many others have resolved to do the same. We are young and strong – and we have the ancestors on our side. Do you not remember Babamunini telling us about the first *chimurenga,* when we first fought the whites? Do you not remember Sekuru Kaguvi, and Chaminuka? That time has come again...."

"But Farai, we failed the last time. What makes you think the whites will not defeat us like they did those warriors from before?"

Farai nodded. "Some of us will bleed," he replied. "Some may lose their lives. But the spirit of the people will not be broken. They defeated us once before, it is true, but we will not be defeated again, not this time."

I felt a rush of pride rise in my chest. Ah, this was the talk of a brave Karanga man, a real man, a fighter. I looked out before me as dusk settled on all I had ever known and loved. I could not let this go. I would not. And, when I looked at my brother, it was with new pride and understanding. "I will support you in any way I can," I said firmly.

Farai's eyebrows shot up. "But what about Baba?" he asked.

"Farai," I replied, "this fight is bigger than you, bigger than me, bigger than Baba. This is our people's fight and I will support it in any way I can, regardless of the consequences."

Farai smiled at me proudly and put his arm around my shoulder. "You are brave, sister," he said. "Brave and strong. If only there were more women like you."

I opened my mouth to speak, to say that there were many more like me, when I heard my name being called. I gasped. It was already dark and the moon was rising, bright and full. Amai would be worried sick – I was never late home!

"Tariro! Tariro!" It was our younger brother, Tendai.

I leapt to my feet and began to make my way down the hill, stumbling on the stones and clumps of grass as I went. More than once I almost fell, but Farai caught me. My heart thumped in my chest like a wild thing. What had happened? Was I in trouble? Was Baba looking for me? Would he suspect what Farai and I had been talking about? I hurried towards Tendai, who was panting, running through the silver-laced trees towards us.

"Tariro!" he cried, breathless. "There you are! I've been looking for you everywhere. You are wanted at home, you must come quickly!"

"Why, Tendai, why?" I asked, grabbing his arm and looking into his face. "What has happened? Is it Amai? The baby?"

But Tendai shook his head, his eyes wide. "No, sister, no! It is Nhamo! Nhamo has come home!"

8
Retribution

My heart skipped a beat and, for a moment, I lost the power to speak.

Tendai tugged at my hand. "Come, sister," he cried. "Baba said for you to come straight away. Hurry!"

He did not have to call me again. The moonlight shone like ribbons through the trees, painting the leaves and the footpath a milky white. We could see our way clearly and we ran all the way back to the homestead, Tendai flying ahead of us.

My thoughts whirled around inside my head. Nhamo was here, at our homestead? So Baba must have found him in Fort Victoria! He must be safe! Were they here to resume the marriage negotiations? But, if that were the case, Nhamo would not have been allowed to come! Did he ask to see me? Had he missed me as much as I missed him? Had he seen me in his dreams as I had seen him in mine? My mind overflowed with questions and I could feel happiness bubbling up inside me.

But when we had almost reached the homestead, I heard a sound that made my blood run cold. I knew something was wrong, very wrong.

It was the sound of women wailing.

Wailing? I thought. *Why are they crying? What has happened?*

We reached the clearing and I saw that the family was gathered around the great fire in the centre of the homestead. Nhamo and his uncle were seated facing my father, so I could not see their faces. His uncle was waving his hands in the air, shouting, his voice hoarse with anguish. MaiNhamo was wailing, her voice the essence of sorrow and loss, rocking back and forth in Amai's arms. Amai's voice joined hers, lower but still audible, just as chilling. *What had happened?*

In the flickering orange light of the flames, I could see Baba, his brow creased, his hands shaking, the shock and sadness in the wide eyes and open mouths of the other wives and their children. They were all looking at Nhamo.

Nhamo's head, usually held so high, was bowed low, and he was wearing European clothes with holes in the arms, cut off at the knees. He looked smaller somehow, more fragile.

Tendai ran forward, pulling me with him. "Here she is," he shouted to Nhamo. "I've brought Tariro!"

Nhamo turned towards Tendai and, in the light of the fire, I saw the swollen jaw, the crooked, broken nose. I saw the scars on his neck. And I saw the eye that faced inwards, while the other wandered, this way and that, unseeing.

A cry clawed at my throat and came out like a tiny, strangled gasp. My Nhamo, he of the brown eyes and warm, loving gaze, robbed of his sight?

He heard me gasp and his head shook a little, before he turned away to face the fire once more.

"See what they have done to my nephew!" shouted Nhamo's uncle. "They have destroyed him! His future! What will he do now? What can he do? He will need to be looked after until the end of his life – he cannot hunt, he cannot mind the cattle, he cannot even plough the fields! I want justice for my brother's son! They cannot do this!" Then he started sobbing, wiping his face with his gnarled old hand.

I could not take my eyes off Nhamo's back – his bowed head and shaking shoulders. I pressed my eyes shut. This could not be happening! But when I opened them again, everyone was still there. The air was still sick with sorrow, the women's voices still moaned, Nhamo's uncle kept sobbing.

Baba sighed and looked around. "We went to see Thompson together. He was very kind, very understanding. He even agreed not to press charges against Nhamo, so that he would avoid going to jail." He looked down and wiped his brow. "But Watson had already meted out his own punishment... Thompson said he was sorry, that there was nothing he could do now..."

Nhamo's uncle spat in disgust. "That Watson! I wanted to wrap my hands around his neck and squeeze the life out of him! Do you know what he said to me when I went to collect Nhamo from the cell where they were holding him? He told me to take my nephew home and bury him, that he was useless now... and that we should all learn a lesson from this!" He choked with fury. "Can you believe that he said that to me? Have you ever heard such wickedness?"

By now, all the children were sniffling, shrinking back from Nhamo's uncle's words. Their mothers shushed them and held them close.

As for me, although I was shocked and saddened, I did not cry tears, not then. I took a step forward.

I was prepared to go to Nhamo, to put my hand on his shoulder and tell him that I still loved him, that I would be his eyes, that I would help him to heal, that I was prepared to love him in spite of everything.

But Baba did not give me a chance to speak before they left. And it was only later, when he told me that he would not be going ahead with the marriage negotiations, that he did not think Nhamo was fit to be my husband, that I began to cry.

9
Farewell

Everything turned grey after Nhamo came back. Yes, he was back home, but to me it was as if he had never returned. After Baba cut off the marriage discussion, Nhamo's uncle and aunt took him to their homestead. They kept him there, nursing his wounds, helping him to come to terms with his condition. They taught one of his youngest nephews, a bright little boy called Tapiwa, how to guide him, how to take him round the homestead, holding his hand, talking to him about what he could see. He took him to relieve himself, he took him to bathe, he helped him to eat, to prepare for bed. I heard all this from Tendai, of course. I was forbidden to go anywhere near him or his family.

"It's not fair on them, Tariro," sighed Amai. "Give them time to get used to the way things are now..."

But *I* could not get used to it. My life had changed so completely, it was as if a dark cloud had come over it, covering everything I had ever loved with shadow. There was no joy in waking up, no pleasure in eating. The tender, green leaves and the ripening corn held no delight for me, even though the harvest was fast approaching, the time of plenty. I no longer laughed at Tendai's little pranks and wild stories; I no longer smiled at my little brothers and sisters when they played their games and chased the chickens; the giggles and girlish games by the riverside left me cold. I grew old.

I became forgetful, careless. When I was left to look after the children, while our mothers went to bathe, they ran around me, wild, screaming, weaving in and out of each other like a swarm of wasps, buzzing with restless life, choking me with the dust of the homestead. I could not make them listen. I could not make them stay. It was only when my father's second wife, Mainini Tambudzai, came back, breathing fire, grabbing arms, pulling ears, her lips held between her teeth, that the children stopped their wild dance. Mainini clicked her teeth at me and sent me to make the *sadza*, frowning.

I prodded the fire, coaxing it back to life, blowing until my eyes watered. Once the fire was hot, I poured water into the pot and measured the mielie-meal into it. But while I stirred the mixture, my mind began to wander, as it so often did.

Why? Why? One word, one question, over and over again.

But I had no answers. When I thought of how my future had appeared before me, swelling with happiness, and how quickly that happiness had been swept away, I could scarcely draw breath.

"Tariro." A voice, dim in the darkness of my mind.

"Tariro." More insistent now, recognisable.

"Tariro!" It was Mainini. "What are you doing? The *sadza* is burning!"

And it was. Furious with myself, I cried bitter tears as I tried to scrape the porridge away from the black bottom of the pot, even as the charred smell filled the hut like a curse. I would have to start again. My hot tears splashed down into the pot.

Mainini shook me by the shoulder. "Tariro!" she shouted. "What is wrong with you these days?"

More tears.

Then her voice softened. "It's Nhamo, isn't it?"

I nodded and fell into her outstretched arms, sobbing. I felt her hands on my back, on my head, hands so like Amai's had been when I was still young and needed her to rock me to sleep. "Why, Mainini?" I sobbed. "Why?"

She sighed. "We have all shed many tears about Nhamo, Tariro, more than you know."

"But not Baba," I choked, my voice smothered by her chest. "Not Baba."

"Tariro," she sighed, "your father is only doing what is best for you. I know you love Nhamo but what can he do for you now? What kind of life could you have with him? He is blind, Tariro, he cannot walk without a guide! He can no longer tend the cattle, or even plough the fields with the women! Don't you see how that changes everything?"

"No," I cried, full of passion. "It doesn't change the fact that I love him and he loves me! I love him even more now."

"Ah, Tariro!" she snapped. "Now you are talking like a foolish girl! Why do you want to throw your life away on this boy? Do you think you are the first girl he has ever courted? Do you think he has not told someone else that he will die unless she comes to his homestead, that he is coming to visit her father, that she must put out the fire in his heart, and say yes, yes, yes? Ha? Do you mean to tell me that your mind is so full of words of love that you cannot think straight?"

I stared at her, shocked. She had never spoken to me like that before. No one had. I could not trust myself to speak.

"Tariro," she continued, "I am telling you this as your Mainini. Forget this boy. He can do nothing for you. Do you think your father was the first man to ask to marry me? Of course not! I even believed that I was in love once. But he was a foolish child, just like I was, so full of dreams and fine words – and nothing in the cattle pen to show for it."

I opened my mouth to protest. How could she compare Nhamo to this boy she had known as a girl?

But she guessed what I was going to say and put her hand to my lips. "Yes, I know your Nhamo is different… *was* different. But now, Tariro, you must wake up. You must be clever. If you marry him, you will be like his slave. You will always be looking after him – and then all his children as well! You will live in poverty, unable to respect him because he cannot keep you, a chief's daughter, in the way you are used to. You may think your love will be enough but, trust me *mwana wangu,* that love will disappear when you have to eat love to quench the hunger in your belly. When your children walk barefoot, no clothes on their backs while others' children have new shoes and go to school. When you have to beg your father for money to pay for the hospital in town. Wake up, Tariro! *Chimuka*! The dream is over. It is time to start living in the real world now."

I stared into the fire, numb. I had no words to counter her rationality, her good sense, her coldness. "I don't care," was all I could say.

She sniffed and got up to go. "I never knew a girl so stubborn. Are you really willing to sacrifice that much for him?" Then she shrugged. "Ah, but if you think it will make you feel better, you must go and see him. To quench one's thirst is to go to the pool. Maybe then you will realise how hopeless your dreams are…" With that, she walked out, clapping her hands to remind the children that she was back and that they had better behave.

I stared after her, a plan forming in my mind.

To quench one's thirst is to go to the pool.

"Come on, Tendai, please!" I was pulling Tendai away from his herd, towards the bushes.

"Ah, sisi, Baba *vachandirova*," he whined, "Baba

will beat me for leaving the cattle."

"Your brothers will keep them safe, Tendai," I snapped, impatient. "This is really important." I paused. "I will let you sleep with my blanket when the weather gets cold...?"

His face lit up then. "Your blanket? The one Babamunini brought you? Really?" He grinned and hopped from one foot to the other, unable to contain the excitement of being the only child on the boys' side with his own blanket. How he would savour that softness, that warmth, when the chilly fingers of winter crept into his room after midnight!

I smiled. "Yes, really, I promise."

"So, what do you want me to do?"

"Go quickly to Nhamo's homestead and tell him... tell him to meet me..."

Tendai's eyes grew large and a wicked grin spread across his face. "Does Baba know about this, Sisi Tariro?"

"No, of course not." I frowned. "And you are not going to tell him... or anyone else, *handiti*?" I shook his shoulder. "Right?"

"Yes, yes, of course," he laughed. "I can keep a secret."

"Yes, I know, that is why I am trusting you –

and giving you my blanket!"

He cackled triumphantly and rubbed his hands together, dancing again.

"OK, OK, calm down and listen carefully. Have Tapiwa bring Nhamo to the baobab tree on the other side of the hill, you know the one? The one between our homesteads, *nhaika*?"

Tendai nodded. "I know the one."

"Tell him to meet me there when the sun is halfway to the horizon, before the boys start to come home with the cattle. And come back and tell me what he says."

"OK," waved Tendai, already jogging away through the grass.

"And Tendai," I called, "Make sure no one sees you!"

He waved again and, in a few moments, he had disappeared from view.

Now all I had to do was wait.

I reached the baobab tree early. The sky was clear, blue, stretching out far above me, the heat shimmering above the earth. I sat with my back against the boabab's enormous trunk, happy for the solid roughness behind me. I was so excited, so nervous, that I wasn't sure whether I would be able to stand upright.

Soon I heard the sound of footsteps coming through the bush. I jumped to my feet and ran behind the tree so that I would not be seen. What if it wasn't Nhamo but someone else? Someone who might report me to Baba?

But then I saw them, the tall, broad-shouldered boy, a stick in his hand, following a youngster with a shiny, bald head. It was Nhamo and Tapiwa. I let out a low whistle, the same whistle we had used when we were courting, the secret signal to let one know where the other was hiding.

Nhamo's head jerked up at the sound of my call and I saw again the sightless eyes. A chill ran through me but I swallowed hard and willed myself to step out from behind the tree. Nhamo's unseeing eyes followed the sound of my feet as they stepped through the dry grass towards him – his hearing had always been excellent. I did not speak until I was standing in front of him, in the clearing beneath the baobab. I put my finger to my lips and motioned Tapiwa to go and keep watch. He ran off obediently, and was soon out of sight among the trees.

Nhamo felt his nephew let go of his hand and looked around uncertainly, calling after him. But then he fell silent and listened. It was as if he could hear my beating heart. He reached out towards me and his fingers touched my collarbone. His breath caught. "Tariro?" he whispered, his voice hoarse with disbelief.

"I'm here, Nhamo," I replied, as I took his hand. "I'm here."

Nhamo's lips quivered as his shaking hands traced my neck, my chin, his fingers lingering over my lips. He kept murmuring my name, over and over again.

"Moyo wangu," he kept repeating. "My heart, my own heart…"

"I'm here, Nhamo," I whispered, my eyes closed. "I'm here."

Moments passed. We stood there like that, palms pressed together, eyes closed, for what seemed like forever. It was as if we did not need words – or sight. I felt Nhamo's pain, his anger, his humiliation, as if they were my own, as if his hands spoke to me. And I knew that he could feel my sadness, my regret and my love through my fingertips. I held on to him, my fingers gripping his, not wanting to let go.

I wanted to stay like that forever.

But he was the first to pull his hands away. "You shouldn't be here," he said, and his voice cracked.

"No, Nhamo," I answered, smiling. "You are wrong. This is where I should be, at your side. Don't you see? I can be your eyes, Nhamo. We can get through this together."

But Nhamo turned away, a frown on his face. "No, Tariro," he said. "I could never ask that of you. You deserve more than that. More than me – more than what I have become."

"What you have become?" I could scarcely repeat the words. How could he not know I saw his heart, his love for me, his humility, his gentleness, his honour? None of that had changed.

"Do you still love me, Nhamo?" I asked, taking his hand again, gently this time.

"More than I have ever loved anyone, more than you will ever know," he replied. "And I would love nothing more than to marry you and make you happy, for you to be the mother of my children, to hear Amai call you *muroora*..."

At these words, my heart soared with delight.

"But it cannot be." He dropped my hand for the second time. "I am not the man you deserve.

You must forget me, Tariro, and continue with your life. You must go now." Tears were slipping down his face as he stepped backwards, away from me, stumbling, his hands spread out to touch a landmark.

My eyes full of tears, I made a move to go to him, but he sensed me approaching and put his arm out to shield himself.

"No, Tariro, please! You must go now." He wiped his face and cleared his throat. "Tapiwa! *Uya kuno*. Come here!" Then he turned to me and spoke clearly, in a new, rough voice. "You must go home, Tariro. You should not have come here. Your father would not be pleased." Then, as I turned away from him, sobbing, he reached out and grabbed my arm, pulled me to him and rasped in my ear, "Forget me, Tariro. Forget you ever knew me. I have nothing to give you now." Tears choked his voice and he released me, almost pushing me away as Tapiwa appeared, looking at us quizzically.

"*Handei*," Nhamo said to him. "Let's go."

Tapiwa reached for his uncle's hand and put it on his slight shoulder. Then he gave me a little wave before walking off into the bush with slow, patient steps.

Nhamo followed him haltingly.

"Nhamo!" I cried. "Wait!" He did not look back. I dropped to my knees, shaking. "Don't do this..." I whispered as he disappeared among the trees. I lowered my head and wept into my hands, my tears soaking the dry leaves below me, sinking into the soil.

For what did the earth care that a young girl was kneeling beneath the baobab tree of her birth, heartbroken, wailing as if someone had died?

10
Change of heart

By the time I returned to the homestead, darkness was falling. I could see Amai in the doorway of the cooking hut, looking out for me anxiously.

"Tariro!" she cried when she saw me. "Where were you? I was worried about you!" Then she looked at my face as the light from the fire lit up my swollen face and bloodshot eyes. "Oh, *mwanangu…*" she murmured, reaching out to me.

I put my arms around her but I did not cry. I had cried enough. Mainini had been right. It was time to face the real world.

"Are you OK, Tariro?" Amai whispered. "Did something bad happen?"

I shook my head. "No, Amai, it's nothing. I'm fine now…"

Amai looked at me for several moments and I put on my bravest face. At last she sighed and went back to stirring the pot on the fire. I gently took the wooden spoon from her and she moved away to sit and rest her feet.

I looked at her closely as I started cutting the *muriwo,* at the lines etched on either side of her mouth, at the dark circles under her eyes. Amai looked so small, so frail, all of a sudden. How had I not noticed? My mind had been so full of my own troubles that I had forgotten how much Amai still needed me.

"How do you feel, Amai?" I asked, realising that I hadn't asked her that in such a long time.

Amai grimaced and placed her hand on her belly, already full and ripe with the baby that was to be born. Perhaps in another one or two months, at the most. "The baby still moves a lot," she panted, breathing through the practice contraction that gripped her womb. "Sometimes I cannot sleep, the baby kicks so hard."

"She'll be a fighter, Amai, just you wait and see…"

Amai looked up at me. "Like her big sister, *nhaika*?"

I nodded and smiled at her. "You must make sure you eat properly, Amai, and rest as much as you can. I am here now. I won't leave you again."

"Baba is eating here tonight," Amai told me. "Make sure you don't cook the *muriwo* for too long – you know he doesn't like it if it is overcooked."

Of course I knew that. But I kept a little *muriwo* on the fire because I knew that both Amai and Farai liked their greens soft and tender, with plenty of salt.

⋘⋘⋘

It was difficult for me to serve Baba but Amai made me do it.

"You can't avoid him forever," she said. "He is still your father."

So I stepped into the house where he was sitting, waiting for his meal. I dropped to my knees and greeted him. He returned my greeting, calm, as if nothing out of the ordinary had ever happened. I offered him a bowl of water to wash his hands, a cloth to dry them with. Then, when he had finished, I placed his plate, steaming, in front of him.

He thanked me, then started to eat, picking up *sadza* with his right hand, then dipping it in the chicken stew Amai had prepared. He put the food in his mouth and chewed, savouring the flavour.

I looked at him out of the corner of my eye.

I could not believe he could be so calm, so aloof. It was as if he did not know that he had hurt me more than words could say. But that was Baba. He hardly had feelings of his own. How could I have expected him to understand those of a fourteen-year-old girl, even if she was his daughter?

I got up to go.

"Tariro."

His voice surprised me and I jumped slightly before turning to him. "Yes, Baba?"

"Have you heard any news of the boy, Nhamo?"

I looked up and saw Baba staring at me. In the shadow cast by the fire, I could not see the expression on his face. I trembled inside. Was he testing me? Did he know that I had seen Nhamo that day? What would he do if he knew that I had disobeyed him? But I knew the answer to that question. There would be no sparing of the cowhide whip if my father found that a child had disobeyed him.

I swallowed hard and said, "I hear that he is doing well, Baba... his nephew Tapiwa is his guide..."

"How do you know? Did you go to the homestead?"

"No, Baba," I replied truthfully. "Tendai told me – he and Tapiwa are friends."

This seemed to satisfy him and he nodded gravely. Then, as he turned his face, I noticed for the first time the anxous groove between his eyebrows, the unhappy set of his chin.

"I'm sorry, Tariro," he said softly, and the quiet honesty of his words moved me to tears, even though I had sworn not to cry any more. "He was a fine young man. I'm sorry things turned out the way they did."

That was all he ever said about it. It was not a lot. But it was enough.

<<<<<<<<<<<<<<<<<<<<

Later that night, Babamunini came to speak to Baba. He did not come alone. Several elders were there too, as well as Farai and the other young men. I saw them from my doorway, their grave faces lit up by the flickering firelight.

I saw my uncle talking, his gestures strong and decisive, his words flying up into the dark leaves above him. "Others have resisted, BabaFarai," he intoned. "We can also. If we don't, we have pronounced a death sentence on ourselves and our families. Can you really live with that on your conscience?"

Baba tried to argue but the men all spoke at once,

urging Baba to change his mind about the move. They talked for a long time. At last, Baba gave in, shaking his head, resigned to our fate, whatever that was.

The next day, Baba sent a message on behalf of his people, a message of defiance. 'We will not leave our ancestral lands, under any circumstances.'

And that night, the cowhide drums throbbed with a fierce, triumphant rhythm and the air was thick with dust, red with the dust of stamping, spinning, pounding feet as we danced our jubilation.

I felt happiness seep into my heart – it had been so long since I had smiled. But I was proud that we were standing up for what was ours. That we had refused to be dictated to. Tomorrow we would begin to bring in the harvest and we would at last taste the fruits of our months of toil.

11
Removal

The morning caught us by surprise. Exhausted by the night's festivities, children sprawled, open-mouthed, their faces stained red with dust, their legs and arms entangled on the reed mats on the floor, sticky with night sweat and the heat of the day. But it was not the crowing of the cockerel that woke us from our heavy sleep, but the rumbling sound of engines, twigs scraping metal, branches snapping.

We jumped awake, disorientated, hearts hammering in tight chests. We wondered at the strange sounds that reverberated in the air of the homestead. We emerged from our sleeping huts, clutching cloths about ourselves, staring in wonder and dismay at the large group of African policemen in khaki uniforms, who stood in a row in front of three trucks with open backs. They were all armed: sticks, *sjamboks*, guns.

In the middle of the row stood Deputy District

Commissioner Ian Watson.

I felt a wave of horror engulf me and I shrank back against the wall of my hut.

But he did not look my way. He called out, in his harsh, strident voice. "You people are breaking the law. This land is no longer available for native occupation. You were warned in advance that you had to move. You chose to disobey orders, orders that come direct from Salisbury. You will now be punished, as all criminals who break the law must be punished."

He barked an order to the Africans on either side of him to move forward.

They did.

And unleashed the wildest terror any of us had ever seen.

I can still see it now; hear it; feel it. The panicked cries that pierced the air as the women ran from the men and their rough, groping hands; the shrill screams of the children as they tried to run to their mothers, flee into the bush, go anywhere to escape these men who flung themselves after us like lions.

My first instinct was to look for Amai but I could not see her. I guessed that she had retreated into her hut and I turned to run to her when I found my way blocked by a policeman carrying a *sjambok*. He grabbed me by my arm, leering at me as I tried to twist away, and raised his arm to bring the whip whistling down towards my legs. A slice of fire seared my calf as I cried out savagely and, with all my strength, bit into to the hand that held my arm. The policeman yelled and cursed and drew back his whip again, his eyes red with rage, his teeth bared like those of a jackal. But before he could bring the whip down, I brought my leg up and kicked him, as hard as I could, in his fleshy stomach. His eyes bulged and let go of me, his arms around his middle, a strange gurgling sound coming from his throat.

Then Farai appeared behind him and pushed him to the ground, and grabbed my hand, pulling me towards the bush. But I pulled in the other direction, away from him.

"No, Farai," I cried, "we must go back to get Amai!"

"The men have gone to fetch their weapons!" yelled Farai. "Go and get Amai and stay with her. I will come back for you!" And he raced off into the bush. Several policemen followed him through the trees.

I turned back towards the homestead and saw that the almost-empty granaries were on fire. Hungry flames licked greedily at the dry grass of the thatch and, in moments, they were engulfed in fierce orange flame, a column of black smoke rising above them.

It did not take long for the huts next to the granaries to catch fire. The crackling, snapping, rushing that filled the air mingled with screams, moans and curses as the policemen flooded the homestead. I saw several of my father's wives being dragged, kicking, through the dust of the homestead to the waiting trucks. Some of the men scooped children up in their arms, oblivious to their screams and dumped them in the open lorries where they cried for their mothers.

Then I saw Mainini, shrieking and spitting like a wildcat, clawing at an officer who was dragging her son by the arm. She jumped on to his back, clawing at his face until he lost his balance and let go of the child's arm. But no sooner had she grabbed hold of her child, than another officer delivered a blow to the back of her head. Without a sound, she sank to the ground. Then the two dragged her by her arms across the rough ground towards the trucks.

I could hear Amai calling to me, but I could not see her in the smoke and mass of running bodies. Then I heard the sound of loud shouts and fierce cries, and stamping, running feet. Through the smoke, I saw the silhouettes of men and saw the glint of *pangas* – sabres – raised knobkerries and sticks. Our men had arrived at last.

The battle was swift and furious. Both sides were invisible, dancing like phantoms in and out of the swirling smoke. Men were cut down, shot, left bleeding on the ground to be trampled by others. Some went to the trucks to liberate those trapped there, but they were felled with police batons.

Then I heard the sound of an engine far behind me and I turned to look out towards the fields. The smoke was not as thick there as the wind was blowing it westwards, towards the other huts. I saw something glinting through the trees and I raced to the edge of the homestead, coughing and choking from the thick black smoke.

And what I saw turned my insides to ice.

One of the machines was in our field. It was scooping up the earth, exposing the plant roots, destroying everything we had worked so hard for.

The green fields – the maize, *rapoko,* my groundnuts, my pumpkins – folded in on themselves, the leaves rustling, jostling each other, the stalks snapping in protest, only to be silenced forever, buried again beneath the dark soil. And then the machine moved on, ploughing up the surrounding fields until all the land was brown again, bleeding green leaves, ripe maize.

At once Amai was at my side, clutching my arm, and a cry stuck in my throat as I stared in disbelief, rooted to the spot, watching the destruction of our harvest.

We heard lowing coming from the cattle *kraal* and heard shots pierce the air. Little Tendai came running, tears streaming down his face.

"Baba! Amai!" he cried. "The cattle! They are killing the cattle!"

At that, the men began to shout and, once again, they were in motion, their weapons held high, running towards the cattle pens. Those of us not already on the trucks were surrounded by policemen who prodded us with their sticks and whips. But they did not move us, not yet. They let us stand there and watch as our worst nightmares came true before our eyes.

From the *kraal*, we heard the sound of shouting, curses and then another shot was fired. But then we saw the cattle that had been spared being driven towards the trucks, surrounded by policemen who bristled with rifles.

Our men trailed behind the cattle, also surrounded

by officers, some of them in handcuffs. Baba and Babamunini held Farai upright as they walked. I did not understand why he was leaning on them, why he looked so deathly pale, but as he drew near, the dark gleam of blood on his arm, the metallic smell of bullets and Farai's moans of pain confirmed my worst fears.

They had shot my brother.

It ended soon after that. They rounded us up and herded us on to the backs of the waiting lorries. Then they moved their bulldozers into our homestead and drove them, shuddering, into our homes. All were reduced to mud brick rubble in minutes. Then they set fire to the grass thatch.

A wail rose up from all of us in the trucks as the fire licked through everything that remained of our lives. Many of us could not bear to watch and the children buried their faces in their hands and hid behind their mothers, huddled on the floor of the trucks.

I will never forget my father's face, as he stared at what had once been his home. A single tear trickled down his cheek – and the light went out of his eyes.

That was the day of the great removal.

<<<<<<<<<<<<<<<<<<<<

The removals spread through our area like a *veld* fire, destroying everything in their path. Nhamo, Rudo, all of them, were herded on to trucks where they were driven, grieving, to their new homes on the Native Reserves. Some tried, valiantly, to resist, as we had, but others saw that there was no use. They tried to protect their families, and salvage their belongings instead. There was mass de-stocking of cattle herds and destruction of crops, whole fields cut down, bulldozed, burnt to the ground.

As they were driven away from their ancestral lands, leaving behind the bones and shrines of their forefathers, their children's umbilical cords, all their sweat and dreams, my people mourned.

Some mourned the homesteads they had built with their own hands, some mourned the loss of their cattle. Others mourned the harvest that would have been. But I did not mourn for those things, not even my piece of land with groundnut and pumpkin.

I mourned the loss of my childhood, the certainty of home, a security that I knew, in my heart of hearts,

I would never feel again.

I cried in Amai's arms, as I felt her shaking, and the baby's insistent kicks through her thin dress.

12
Hunger

I put my hand to the earth and picked up a handful of soil.

Sandy. Dry. Tired.

This soil had none of the richness of the fertile land back home. The dry grass that lined the footpath and the wilting maize plants with their desiccated tassels told me that, here, the rains had not been good at all.

In accordance with the Native Land Husbandry Act, the Native Reserves were divided between land that could be cultivated and land for grazing. We had never farmed this way before – it was our practice to rotate the way land was used: this year, cultivation, the next year, grazing. And, in the old days, when the land grew tired, people moved on to fresh land while the old fields restored themselves.

But in what was now Rhodesia, there was no way of moving on when the fields ceased to produce.

Most of the land, the best land, would never belong to us now. The whites had taken a map of the country and divided the land – our land – among themselves, leaving us with the drought-stricken, tired land, in the driest, hottest areas, home to tsetse flies and slow starvation.

We knew immediately, as soon as we arrived, that this was a place of death. We saw it in the listless gait of the men who loitered around their homesteads, sitting in front of hastily built houses that were too close together, rubbing shabby shoulders with their neighbours, jostling for space, where once there had been so much. We saw it in their hostile, accusing eyes – we had come to make their lives harder, with less land to go around and more mouths to feed.

We saw it in the dark circles under the wary eyes of the women who stared at us as we filed past, their dresses torn and dirty, their hair unkempt, flies buzzing round the half-closed eyes of the babies they carried so carelessly on their backs.

We saw it in the reddish tinge of the children's hair and their round, distended bellies that protruded above scab-ridden legs, spindly and bowed with malnutrition.

The smell of hunger, disease and death clung

to everything. And, slowly, it began to claim us too.

I first noticed it with Amai. All of us were subdued when we arrived, all of us held hearts full of pain and fear about the future. But it seemed that, with Amai, the wounds remained raw for many weeks so that, even after everyone else had asserted a kind of rhythm, established a vaguely familiar routine, Amai still could not settle.

Her cheekbones grew sharper than before and her eyes appeared to sink into their sockets, giving her a haunted look. She slept badly and, sometimes, her hands shook uncontrollably and I was gripped by fear. What was happening to my mother?

I was not the only one to notice how thin and frail she had become, so thin that it looked like she would not be able to carry the weight of the baby inside her. So we all made sure that she rested as much as possible. Baba came to visit her every day but, out of consideration for her condition, spent the night at one of the other houses.

Farai's gunshot wound was treated and he healed well. He was soon able to participate in the building of the new houses, along with the other men, while we cut dry grass from the surrounding bush to use as thatch.

He, Garikai and my other siblings all came to visit Amai at least once a day, enquiring after her health, asking if they could do anything. The visits seemed to cheer her and my younger siblings, especially Mainini Tambudzai's children, never failed to put a smile on her face. Her best friend, MaiNhamo, found a way to come and she brought Rudo. Of course, we did not openly speak of Nhamo but his mother told us that they had been moved to another reserve a few kilometres away. They too had tried to refuse to leave but had been overcome. Their conditions seemed just as bleak as ours. Later, Rudo and I went for a walk and I was able to articulate the question that had been burdening my brain for the longest time, ever since we had arrived at that place.

"How is Nhamo, Rudo?" I asked. I noticed, with slight surprise, that my heart still fluttered when I spoke his name. Of course, he often visited my dreams and made me hope again. But, in the morning, I would wake up depressed and heavy-hearted, and I would prepare the water for the day with a stoop to my shoulders.

I had so many regrets. But life, in its present form, had taken over, and there was precious little time to daydream of childhood sweethearts in this place where, it seemed, love had never bloomed at all. So saying his name out loud to Rudo – the only person I could mention him to, aside from Amai – was both a relief and a strain. Too many regrets.

"Nhamo is doing well," Rudo replied. "It has taken him some time to adjust to the new surroundings but he's learning to use a stick to guide himself, becoming more independent. He is determined not to be a burden, he says."

"That is good," I breathed, thinking of him bathing, eating, washing his hands, in the dark, and feeling that wellspring of guilt and shame bubble up inside me. "Does he ever..?"

Rudo smiled. "Of course," she said, looking at me kindly, "all the time. But he told me never to tell you, so you don't know, OK?"

I nodded, then looked around at the new huts that were being built, the bare fields beyond. "I think he is lucky," I said quietly.

"Lucky?" she said, puzzled. "What do you mean?"

"Without sight, Nhamo will never know how terrible this place really is. How unlike home. He will always hold his true home in his mind's eye – he will never have to look at the ugliness and squalor of these settlements. For us… it is not so easy."

"Home?" whispered Rudo, a tear creeping into her eye. "I don't think any of us will be able to hold on to what was home, not for very long."

"Do you not think the land stays with you?" I asked. "Do you not think that the place of your ancestors, the place where your umbilical cord is buried, will always have a hold on you?" I closed my eyes tight, to stop the tears that threatened to fall. "I don't know whether I will ever know home again. I don't know whether I can put down roots anywhere else…."

Rudo nodded, understanding me at last, and we both gazed miserably at the scrawny chickens that scratched at the hard-packed earth.

"Baba says that Thompson has promised things will get better here – more food, water, medicine…" My voiced trailed away. Baba had lost the respect of the clan and, with it, his credibility.

But Rudo was too kind to say anything about that. All she did was shrug and get to her feet, dusting off the back of her faded purple dress. "*Totenda maruva tadya chakata*," she said simply. "We will believe in the blossoms when we eat the fruit."

So, life continued. We were allocated land and told to make sure we kept the cattle on the pasture used for grazing. But even though large numbers of our herd had been killed before we left our old homestead, the new fields still weren't big enough to prevent overgrazing.

Our new plots were also much smaller than we were used to but we made do. We hoed the light, sandy soil, hoping always to reach the dark, fertile soil beneath the sandy surface.

But we never did.

So we planted seed given to us by Thompson's men and listened as they lectured us on the correct use of fertiliser and warned us not to plant by the streams. But no one was interested in planting on the river bank. As soon as we reached the settlement, we heard stories of how some men, no one knew which ones or where they were from, were known to frequent the river, waiting for young girls who had come to draw water or wash clothes or bathe. These men used to spy on the girls when they bathed and, if their proposals of love were not accepted, they sometimes took what they wanted without asking.

"You must never go to the stream on your own, Tariro," Amai warned. "Always take one of the boys with you, or go with Mainini."

"Yes, Amai," I answered. "Of course."

By this time, Amai was confined to her hut. The baby was due so soon and her discomfort was so intense, it was decided that she should rest completely until the baby came. I started sleeping in her hut again, just as I had as a very young girl.

One night, as we settled down to sleep, Amai reached over the blankets and took my hand. Hers was so small, the fingers so thin and frail that I hardly recognised them.

Amai began to speak, her voice a soft whisper. "Tariro," she began, "have I ever told you the story of your birth?"

I smiled to myself. It had indeed been a long time since Amai had told me the story of my birth beneath the baobab tree. I yearned to hear the familiar tale again, to return once more to a time of safety and knowing, a time of peace.

And so it began. Amai told me how she had been heavy with child, craving the fruit of the baobab. She spoke of the birthing pains that forced her to her knees, how she came to realise that she was not going to make it to the homestead.

"Then I knew that the ancestors meant for me to give birth to you on my own. And I did, I did. I never felt so strong, so brave, before or since. My daughter, my daughter, the only one who stayed with me… the only one…" She was crying and so was I, tears that stung my eyelids before spilling over and running down my cheeks and into my ears. Amai leaned over and hugged me awkwardly, across the mountain of unborn baby.

"Why, Amai?" I murmured. "Why are you telling me this now?"

"To keep the story alive, Tariro. To keep our history alive. So that, one day, you can tell your own daughter about how you were born at the foot of that baobab tree… so she will know where she comes from. So she will be able to find her roots."

Then Amai began to sing to me, a soft, sweet song that stirred within me echoes of childhood, of days spent on my mother's back. I was soon lulled into a deep, peaceful sleep, the first I had had in months.

It was her voice that woke me. A low, tortured moaning drifted towards me and, as it increased in volume and anguish, snatched me from sleep with a jolt.

"Amai?" My eyes searched the dark when my hands failed to find her lying beside me.

"Tariro…" her voice was a hoarse whisper, haunted. It chilled me to the bone.

"Amai," I called out and, on my knees, felt my way to her. I found her on her side, trembling, her teeth chattering although it was a warm night. How long had she been this way? How long had I been sleeping? How soon was the dawn? I had no way of knowing from the dark within and the blackness outside.

Amai's bony fingers gripped my shoulder and I put my arm around her, trying to soothe her.

"What is it, Amai?" I asked. "Is it the baby?" I could feel her taking panting breaths and then she tensed and I could feel the contractions gripping her belly through her wrapper. The baby was on its way! I started to get up so that I could rush for Mainini and the midwife, but Amai pulled me to her.

"Tariro," she rasped, "I never told you about my dream. I didn't want you to worry. But now,

now I feel I must tell you. I must warn you."

My blood ran cold. Amai's dreams were well-known for their accuracy. It was said that the spirits told their stories to her in the night, whispering to her of glad tidings or impending disaster.

"This baby will not live, Tariro," she choked. "It is another ghost child. I saw it, saw it clearly. The stream, the stream was red with blood and the baby was white like a ghost, with blue, blue eyes. And I was standing in the stream and the baby came and the stream washed it out, washed it away. Washed it away, Tariro. And the blood flowed and flowed, Tariro, until it washed me away too..." Her voice was drowned by her sobs.

Stricken, I faced her. "No, Amai," I almost shouted, disguising my horror at her words. "This baby will live! There is no stream, no blood. Just a baby who wants to come out. You must be strong, Amai, please, and don't think about this dream, this evil dream. It means nothing..." But even to my own ears the words sounded hollow. I had to get help.

Amai's moans had turned to deep, guttural sounds, completely different from her normal voice. It was as if she was possessed.

Terrified, I told her to hold on and dashed out

of the hut, over to Mainini's hut.

"Mainini, Mainini! *Mukai*!" I called out, my panic-stricken voice betraying mey fear. "Amai has gone into labour! She needs the *muchingi*! The baby is coming now!"

Within moments, Mainini was up and out of her house, tying a scarf firmly on her head, adjusting her waist-wrapper, carrying a candle. She woke Baba and told him to send for the midwife immediately. Then she flew to the hut where Amai's cries filled the enclosed space with hysteria. By the light of the candle, I saw my mother on all fours, her face contorted in pain, sweat glistening on her forehead. Her lips looked bruised, her eyes were bloodshot.

Immediately, Mainini was on the floor next to her, talking to her, soothing her, adjusting her wrapper, trying to make her comfortable. But I could see the worry in her eyes, the nervous way she felt Amai's stomach when it stiffened.

"Tariro," she said to me, "go and fetch water. Lots of it."

"Mainini," I began, "I want to stay…"

"Just go, Tariro!" Mainini shouted, her voice edged with something I couldn't name. Was it irritation? Anger? *Fear*?

Eyes welling up, I nodded and stumbled out of the hut. I knew that Mainini kept a drum of water in her kitchen so I went there, lit a match, and fumbled for a bucket.

When I stepped back into the hut with the bucket of water, I saw that the midwife had not yet arrived.

Mainini was squatting by Amai, her forehead and upper lip beaded with sweat. "Come on," she was saying, "come on!" She had one hand on Amai's belly, the other between her legs.

Amai's face was drawn, her eyes rolled back in her head, her breathing was shallow. She looked as if she was ready to give up.

But Mainini shouted at her, "Push now, MaiFarai! Push, or you will lose this baby!"

That was just what Amai needed to hear. With one last effort, she bore down, a shuddering cry wracking her body.

In that moment, I saw Mainini pull and there was the baby, screaming, gleaming, steaming with life. Mainini let out a ragged sigh, smiled broadly, and handed the baby to me to cover with a blanket.

"Well done, MaiFarai," she smiled and ululated softly. *"Makorokoto mwana mutsva…"*

I was smiling too, smiling so much I thought my heart would burst. I looked into my little sister's face: the pinched features of a newborn, the tiny, perfect mouth, opening and closing as it searched for milk. My heart turned somersaults and flew out of the window to dance with the stars. I had never seen anything so beautiful in all my life. My sister. My long-lost, longed-for sister. My mind filled with one thought: Amai's dream had been wrong. The ancestors had let this one go.

I turned, beaming, to show the baby to Amai, expecting to see her eyes light up, to see a smile touch her face at the sight of her daughter, to see her forget the pain of the birth and feed her child.

But what I saw then will stay with me forever.

Amai was lying back, her face turned towards the light. Her skin was grey, her mouth open, as if in wonder. Her eyes were closed. Disbelieving, I looked towards Mainini and saw her gaze with horror at the floor in front of her.

Blood. My mother's blood.

Oh, Amai's blood was flowing, flowing, like a stream, into the crevices of the dirt floor. And it didn't stop. It just kept flowing like a river.

I felt a cry rise in my throat and I threw myself at my mother's leaden body, grabbing her, shaking her to make her wake up, sit up and see the baby. Just to open her eyes.

"Amai, wake up!" I screamed, over and over again until Mainini pulled me away, her face wet with tears. Her dress, her hands, the cloth she held, were all soaked with my mother's blood.

"Stop, Tariro," she choked. "She is gone..."

The pain sliced me like a *panga*, shredding my insides with grief. No! No! A thousand times no!

Amai, oh, Amai...

"Maiweeee...." A thin wail came from my throat as I rocked with my baby sister in my arms, holding her close. Then lifting her away from me to see her face again, seeing the eyes, closed so peacefully, and the little body, limp in my arms.

And realising that she too was gone.

Amai and her longed-for daughter were finally together.

It was the raw pain and grief of my cry that brought the rest of the family stumbling out of sleep to Amai's hut.

13
Invasion

The grass crackled as I made my way down the patchy, grey-grassed hillside to the stream that struggled through the valley. With poor rains, I knew it was going to be hard to fetch water that was not red with mud, clogged with stones and debris.

But I had to try. Tendai was ill and his fever needed to be cooled with water, a lot of it.

Amai and the baby had been gone for three months and still death continued to stalk us. We had buried Amai and the baby together and done all the necessary rituals. The beer had been brewed and her cow – the *mombe yeumai* – was safely in the cattle kraal.

Amai's absence was like a physical ache. Not a day went by when I did not long for her or expect to turn round and find her there, pounding the dried maize to make *upfu*, plucking a chicken. While we worked in the fields, I found myself opening my mouth to call out to her, to tell her that I would try planting pumpkin again, that the goat had nibbled at the maize plants because one of the younger boys had let it run off.

Then I would remember and close my mouth. And whatever hope or joy that was about to bubble up would grow quiet and still, until the whole world became a place of sad memories and arduous chores.

All I wanted to do was sleep – and dream. For that was when I felt close to Amai: when her spirit visited me.

She did not say anything.

She was just there.

And that was enough.

It took Tendai's illness to wake me out of my stupor. Baba and the older boys had gone to town to try to get medicine for Tendai, and Mainini was left to care for him.

Poor Mainini. She tried her best to look after us while mourning Amai, but the strain was showing.

So I knew I had to be the one to fetch water for Tendai – there was no one else.

I walked as quickly as I could, balancing my pot on my head, listening out for any unfamiliar sounds. But all I heard was the call of the fish eagle and the distant lowing of the cattle.

Soon enough I reached the stream. My brow furrowed as I looked at the sluggish water. I hadn't collected water in months – was this all there was? This water would only make Tendai's condition worse. Perhaps if I walked upstream, I would find a place where the water ran more freely than here, where the water settled in stagnant pools which would, in time, become a breeding ground for mosquitoes.

I began to walk, watching the water – its colour, the way it moved. It seemed to be getting clearer as I walked. If only I could go a little further, I would be closer to the source, and I would be able to fill my pot with cool, clear water for my brother, Tendai.

Then I found the place. There, in the shade of the msasa trees, the stream had become a pool, bound on either side by rocks. Here the water was clear and the sandy bottom gleamed as the sun dappled through the tree leaves.

I sank gratefully to my knees and scooped the

water with my cupped hands, brought it to my mouth. On tasting it, I sighed with relief. Yes, this was the water I had been looking for. Glancing up, I saw that the sun was low, much lower than it had been when I left the homestead. Quickly, I filled the water pot from the pool and, adjusting the support, lifted the pot on to my head. I would need to hurry now to make it home before sunset – Mainini would be worried about me. Deftly, steadying the pot with one hand, I began to walk quickly along the riverbank, following the water back downstream.

But just as I reached a bend in the stream, I heard a crackling sound, like a heavy foot on msasa tree pods. I turned sharply towards the sound but saw no one. I thought perhaps I had been mistaken. I turned back and continued walking, straining my ears to catch any more strange sounds.

Then I heard it again.

I whirled round and peered into the thick trees on the other side of the stream. I was sure that was where the sound had come from, but still I could see nothing. Then, just as I turned away, I saw what looked like a man's shadow move between the trees.

"*Ndiani*? Who's there?" I called out, thinking maybe it was Farai or Garikai playing a joke on me, trying to scare me. But then I remembered that they had all gone into town.

And suddenly I remembered what the villagers had told us about the men by the stream. I shuddered and stepped forward. No sooner had I done so when three men – strangers – stepped out from behind the msasa trees on the other side of the stream.

They were wearing patched khaki shorts and wore no shoes on their feet. Two of them had no shirts and their bare chests glistened with sweat, tight curls sprouting across them like peppercorns. The third wore a khaki shirt and was carrying a young buck across his shoulders. It was still bleeding and the blood from its wound spread across the shoulder of his khaki shirt. They had been hunting. They all stood there, staring at me. My heartbeat quickened as I looked into their faces, looking for reassurance, sensing danger. I faltered before greeting them, as was customary when meeting elders, even ones you didn't know. But they didn't answer. They just kept staring at me, fire burning in their eyes, the air vibrating with tension. I swallowed hard, and made to walk on.

And, in that moment, a horse stepped out into the open and there, astride it, sitting loosely in the saddle with a rifle slung across his shoulder and a *sjambok* in his hand, was Deputy District Commissioner Ian Watson.

I felt my insides curdle like sour milk at the sight of his red skin, his now crooked nose (oh, Nhamo!) and the icy blue eyes, eyes that swept over me and, settling on my face, flashed with recognition. A slow smile slid across his face and I looked away immediately, feeling dread trickle through me.

He walked his horse slowly to the side of the stream and called out to me. "Hello there," he said, smiling, showing a row of even, white teeth. The way he smiled reminded me, once again, of a crocodile, grinning, waiting for its prey to come close, to be dragged down to the watery grave of the riverbed.

I said nothing but remained rooted to the spot.

"So, we meet again," he said casually. "Where are you going, all on your own? Would you like some company?"

I could hear from the tone of his voice that he was asking me questions and I shook my head. I did not dare look at him this time but began walking along the riverbank, my trembling hands holding on to my water pot. Out of the corner of my eye, I could see Watson on his horse, keeping pace with me.

He was still talking, asking me my name in

broken Shona. He made his voice sound smooth and sweet, as if he was talking to a child, or coaxing a calf that had taken fright and refused to come out of the kraal. But I carried on walking, willing myself home. Because I could not remember where I had begun my journey; everything looked so different in the fading light. Behind me, I could hear the men's feet sloshing through the muddy water. They were now on my side of the stream. They followed me, unhurried, waiting to see what their master wanted them to do.

At last, Watson stopped his horse and his voice changed. "Hey you!" he shouted, his voice returning to the harshness I knew so well. "I'm talking to you!" Then he drew himself up in his saddle. "Come here," he ordered, his voice imperious, his tone assured, knowing that, because of the colour of his skin, I was obliged to obey his command immediately.

The side of me that was scared, hungry, grieving, the side of me that remembered the feel of his fist in my face, pushed me to obey him. I almost did. But there was still a flame inside me, a tiny, flickering flame, a flame of dignity, honour, even bravery, that refused to be cowed. I would not go willingly towards humiliation. I had not forgotten what he had done to Nhamo. I had a pot of clean water on my head and my brother was waiting for me. I lifted my head and began to walk towards home, my heart showing me the way.

This seemed to send Watson into a rage. "I said come here, damn it!" he shouted.

That was when I began to run.

I ran awkwardly, trying to keep the pot of water on my head, the water leaping over the sides, running down my raised arms. As soon as I started running, I heard Watson click his teeth at his horse and swear loudly. He shouted an order to the other men behind me and brought his whip down hard on his horse's rump. The beast whinnied and reared up. Then the horse broke into a gallop, its hooves churning up the earth on the edge of the stream. Behind me, I could hear the men running, their feet heavy on the soft earth, their panting breaths growing closer.

Ahead of me, I saw Watson pull hard on the horse's reins and wheel it into the stream and up the opposite bank, cutting me off from the path homeward. That was when I finally threw down the half-empty water pot and plunged into the bush.

The moments that followed were a blur. The sunlight had now faded and everywhere, shadows lurked. I ran, small cries escaping my lips, dodging trees, jumping over low-lying shrubs, tearing my skin and clothes on thorns and grasping branches. But I did not stop. My blood roared in my ears and my heart thumped about in my chest like a wild thing, trapped too long, gone mad.

Through the din, I could hear Watson calling to his men, and I could hear them crashing through the dry leaves, shouting to each other, gaining on me. But I did not stop. I ran for my life, even as the air burned in my lungs and I felt lightness flood my head. I had not eaten properly for three months and my strength was not what it was. But I did not stop.

And I did not see the tree.

The tree with the low branches, wide and spreading, reaching. I did not know it was there until I ran into it and felt myself fall backwards from the impact.

They were on me in a moment. These three anonymous men, men who could have been my uncles, my older brothers, grabbed at my arms and legs with rough, weather-beaten hands. I was wild with terror, trying to swallow the dryness from my throat, trying to look them in the eyes. I began to talk to them in our language, plead with them in the name of their mothers, the ancestors, anyone. My words came out too fast, burbling like a hot spring, coloured by tears.

"Please, my fathers," I begged, tears streaming down my face as I struggled against their iron grip. "Please let me go. Please! Don't do this!"

But they refused to look at me. Holding me from behind, the one with the blood-stained shirt told me to shut up.

Then madness overtook me. I began to scream.

I screamed for my mother, my father, my brothers, a wild, anguished scream that betrayed the depths of my fear, of my powerlessness. But the blood-stained one clamped his hand over my mouth and my cries were muffled, echoing only in my head. I tasted sweat, metal, blood.

Then, through trees touched by twilight, Watson appeared. His gun gleamed in the new moonlight. His eyes flashed, blue, blue, blue. I squeezed my eyes shut as he came towards me and reached out a hand. I felt his finger trace the line of my jaw.

"There, there," he was crooning. "That's better. I told you I didn't want to hurt you..."

I struggled against the men again, my feet drumming on the earth, trying to draw as far away from him as possible.

Watson chuckled softly, as if to himself. "*Ja*, you've got spirit," he murmured. "I remember from the last time we met. That's good." And he put down his rifle.

My eyes flew open and widened in horror when I saw what he intended to do. I thrashed out again, ready to fight to the end. But my limbs were weak with hunger, my legs leaden with too much sorrow and I could not withstand the blow that he aimed at my right temple. My body slumped, despair flooding me at last.

"You boys wait for me with Millie, by the stream," he said to the others. "Go now!" And they melted into the dusk.

Then Watson grabbed me by my shoulder. He pushed me roughly to the ground. Panting, his sweat dripping on to me, he crushed my face into that unfamiliar soil and took from me what I had been saving for Nhamo, my childhood sweetheart.

After he had gone, I lay there in the dark, broken, bleeding, surrounded by the deafening screech of crickets, haunted by the call of a night owl. I wanted to bury my face in the soil and never, never see the light of day again.

14
Confinement

Farai found me the next day, after having looked for me all night. I heard him calling me from a long way away but the dryness in my throat, the blood caked on my parched lips, and my voice, hoarse and weak from the screaming before and the crying afterwards, would not let me answer him. It was only when he came nearer that he was able to find the source of the anguished whimpers.

On seeing me lying, twisted, among the fallen leaves and dew-damp bushes, my brother's eyes grew wide with shock and fear. He knelt beside me, his hands raised in front of him, wanting to lift me but not knowing how, where to touch me. He could not help but stare at my cuts, my bruises, the blood that had crusted on my temple where Watson had struck me.

"Wh-wh-who did this to you, Tariro?" he

stammered, anguish echoing in his voice, in the way he blinked and blinked, not wanting to look at my torn clothes, my exposed legs.

I tried to turn away to hide the tears that oozed out from under my swollen eyelids, but I could not turn my head – the night cold and the morning dampness had seeped into my bones and stiffened my muscles, as in death. So my brother could only bow his head to hide his own tears when the dry moans began in my throat and reverberated through my aching body.

"Leave me," I groaned. "Just leave me here to die, Farai."

But he picked me up in spite of my cries, and carried me up the parched hill, over the dusty homestead floor, to my home.

"Mainini!" Farai's voice was dark and thick with tears. "*Uyai kuno*! Come quickly!"

Mainini came running out, her baby on her hip. But when she saw me, the dark bruises that bloomed on my legs and arms, my battered face, the blood on my clothes, she let the baby slide to the floor as she fell to her knees, her hands raised to her head, her face disfigured with grief. She began to wail, a terrible, piercing sound that brought everyone out to see what had happened, what new tragedy had struck our family.

"*Maiwee*!" she screamed, over and over again, tearing at her dhuku, striking her face, rocking her body to and fro. "*Mwana wangu*! *Yowee*! They have killed my child! They have killed my child! Baba waFarai, come and see! Come and see what they have done to your child!"

Her voice was joined by others, shrill, disbelieving. I heard a child's whimpering cry, a mother's shushing, sensed bodies pressing into the air around me, smelt the dust raised by many feet, the smell of early morning breath, exhaled in shock and disbelief. Someone covered me with a blanket and I felt Farai's arms twitch with the effort of holding me up, of containing his anger and grief.

At last, I heard Baba's voice, sombre, with a tremble around the edges. "Take her inside, Farai," he said. "Everyone move back, move back… she needs rest. She needs plenty of rest…."

But Mainini sprang to her feet and, through my barely-open eyelids I saw her grab on to his faded overalls, her eyes wild. "See what they have done to your child!" she hissed, the veins in her neck bulging obscenely. "See what they have done to her? They will not stop! Never! This is what they began when they took our land – and they will never stop!"

Baba just gazed at her, a frown on his face. She had forgotten herself. He moved to remove her hand from his chest but she snatched it away before he could touch her.

She began to back away from him, pointing her finger accusingly. "You refused to stand up when they destroyed that young man, Nhamo! You refused to stand up when they came for the land! Now, they have stolen your daughter's honour, her innocence! And still you stand calmly, speaking of rest? No!" Her voice was shrill as she spat out her caustic words. "A thousand times no! This cannot be borne with patience! This is the time for action! For vengeance!"

I saw Baba draw himself up, aware of the stares of his family, hard on him and his wife. He gave her a warning look and clenched his fist. "MaiTsiti," he said in a low voice. "You go too far."

"Too far?" her voice mocked, laughed and cried, all at once. "I have not gone far enough! Was it a man that I married, or a mouse, too afraid of the white man to defend his family's honour? Eh? What kind of man are you? What kind?"

Baba's hand appeared from nowhere, knocking Maimini across her mouth, sending her sprawling in the dust. A great moan rose up from everyone – wives, children, passers-by who had come to see what the wailing had been about.

Baba stood over Mainini, trembling with fury. "Never," he muttered between clenched teeth, "never speak to me like that again. Or you will regret the day you left your mother's womb!" With that, he turned on his heel and stalked away. As he passed me, he barked to Farai to take me inside and for Garikai to accompany one of the other children to fetch water so that I could bathe.

But all the water in the stream would never cleanse me. They could bathe my wounds, wash the grass and dust out of my hair, scrub the sand, skin and blood from under my nails, but it would never be enough. I would never be clean again, not even if they used all the water in the Save River.

I would never be whole again. I had been violated in the worst way, by the man I hated most in the world – the one who had stolen the man I loved more than anything. They say that time heals, but I knew then that I would never be able to cleanse my mind of the memory of his eyes, his cruel smile, his grasping hands…nor my ears from the echo of his voice, taunting me.

And who would protect me at night, when he came to me in my dreams, on his horse, stalking me through the trees, like the leopard stalks its prey, claiming me as his own? Who would keep me safe?

No one.

That was what made me cry the most.

And I shed more tears when weeks passed and I remained clean. When nausea gripped me as the cock crowed in the early morning yard. When my waist began to thicken. When I knew that my nightmare was far from over. When I realised that Watson had left me with more than cuts, bruises and nightmares. When I knew that he had left me to carry his seed. And, as I felt the baby move inside me, I could do nothing but picture his blue, blue eyes and weep for the life I carried inside me.

I could do nothing but weep for this child born of violence and hatred.

For this child born of shame.

15
Prophecy

Against my wishes, Watson's child grew inside me, binding herself to me. Against my will, my body nourished her, cradling her as she grew. She shared my air, followed my every movement and, when she moved for the first time, she captured my heart, filling me with wonder, against my will. I knew then, with bruising certainty, that I would love this child, in spite of the manner of her conception. My blood ran through her veins, she held part of my spirit. She was a part of me.

And I knew, with equal certainty, that she would be a girl.

But no one understood my feelings. I had to suffer the shame of carrying a child when no one had paid *roora* for me. Those girls I had known by the riverside where we had washed clothes together, now tore me to shreds with their whispers and suspicions.

Baba bore the humiliation with characteristic silence, a silent dignity that, for the first time, made me respect him. He refused to cower before the wagging tongues of the villagers and he made a point of going to Fort Victoria to tell Thompson what Watson had done, that his daughter was carrying Watson's child. Babamunini went with him.

I went also.

Of course, they advised against it.

"Why upset yourself any further?" asked Baba.

But Babamunini understood. "Sometimes," he said, "the only way to have peace is to face your enemies…."

It was my first time going into the town. I had oiled my arms and legs and wore the new pink dress that Babamunini had bought me. But still, it stretched painfully over my swollen abdomen. I tied my waist wrapper over it, trying to hide it a little. Then we rode the bus to town, crushed by crying children, anxious passengers and goats.

Fort Victoria was intimidating. I had never seen so many people, so many cars, so many *varungu*. They walked the streets and drove in their cars, confident and aloof, their black servants carrying their bags. There were places where blacks weren't allowed to sit, weren't allowed to eat, weren't allowed to be. Babamunini explained the signs that said 'Whites only'.

We passed a trading store. There was a white family standing next to a truck – the man wore a bush hat on his head and shorts that showed his hairy legs; the woman wore a flowery dress with a belt. Black workers were hauling huge sacks of grain and other supplies on to the back of the truck. The children were licking something white that they held with a stick. The white substance dribbled down their fingers and chins. They looked happy and well-fed.

"Farmers," said Babamunini, looking at them. "Many of them have made good money from the land they stole…."

I looked at them darkly. A family like theirs was probably farming on our land now. It made my blood boil.

"You see those children?" he said, pointing to a group of white children dressed in smart dresses, jackets and socks that came up to their knees. "They go to a school especially for white children. Blacks can't send their children there, even if they have the money."

Later, I was to see the school for the black

children – a long, low building with a corrugated-iron roof set in a dusty yard, surrounded by a sagging, wire fence. The children looked happy to be going to school, but I noticed that their uniforms were faded and patched and that many of them had no shoes.

And inside I burned with the injustice of it all.

When we reached the District Commissioner's office, we had to wait a long time before Thompson would see us. By that time, my feet were aching and I was very thirsty. I asked the secretary if I could have a drink of water as I saw that she had a jug of water with a glass on the desk beside her. She looked at me and raised her eyebrows, then pointed outside.

I went outside and saw nothing but a metal tap that the gardener was using to water the garden through a long hose. I realised that this was where she considered me fit to drink from. And although my mind was bruised by this indignity, it didn't stop me drinking from the hose, or washing my face with the cool water.

When I came back in, I saw her look at me, disgusted. But I didn't care.

Of course, when we finally saw him, Thompson expressed his regret, his frustration at his deputy's wild ways colouring his cheeks. Yes, he knew that this kind of thing was happening, yes, he would talk to Watson. No, no chance of criminal charges, no witnesses, government's reputation and so on, you understand.

"He's leaving the job anyway," Thompson added. "He's got himself some land not too far from here, getting married and all that. I think that will settle him down. You won't have to worry about him any more…"

But Babamunini looked at him hard, raised his voice and continued to wrangle with him until Thompson offered to pay us an amount of money in compensation. It was not a lot but it was something, something to put away for the baby's medical bills, for school.

Then, just as we were leaving the office, I saw him.

He was parking his car and there was a young woman with yellow hair and red lips with him. He was teasing her and she was laughing, in the way that only a woman in love can. I left Baba and Babamunini as they walked towards the road and approached the car. I stood still, next to the window, waiting for Watson to see me.

And when he did, he recognised me, and his

blue, blue eyes widened as he saw my swollen belly. I saw him redden and hesitate before turning back to his lady friend. I stayed there, even while my father called my name; I stayed there looking at Watson, accusations and curses burning in my eyes.

At last I heard the white woman say, "Does that *kaffir* girl know you? She keeps staring…"

"No," Watson growled, never once looking my way, "of course not."

Oh, but I did. I did.

And I swore that, before I died, I would face ex-Deputy District Commissioner Watson again. And the next time, I would not keep silent.

<<<<<<<<<<<<<<<<<<<<

My little girl was born that year, at the end of a long drought. The first drops of hoped-for, longed-for, prayed-and-danced-for rain began to fall as I felt my womb contract with a new urgency. The pain was muted by the elation that danced on the air, the air that sighed and shivered at the caress of the rain, having stood, dry and still, for so long. This was the long-awaited end of the dry season.

I gave birth with Mainini at my side, my cries

muffled by the thundering rain outside the hut, the fierce showers that turned the dust of the homestead to mud, driving brick-red rivulets down the hill to fill the parched stream with fresh vigour. The stream that grew so ecstatic that it overflowed and broke its banks

When my baby first tasted the close, woody air and cried out, the midwife handed her to me. I held her steaming, squirming little body in my arms, trembling, tears mingling with sweat on my face, amazed at what my body had brought forth.

Then she opened her eyes and stared up at me.

I flinched.

Her eyes were blue, blue. Just like her father's.

Had it not been for the nine months of love that had taken root in my heart, I would have turned away then. I would have handed her back to the midwife and seen her open her eyes wide, her hand to her mouth, shock and incomprehension etched on her face.

Had it not been for the fact that I loved her.

Instead, I looked deep into those blue, blue eyes and saw my mother's warmth and strength shining back at me. This baby's eyes were wise and gentle, just like Amai. My tears fell as I caressed her cheeks, as smooth as pebbles, and touched my little finger to her dark lips as she searching for me. I held her to me, crying for the surge in my heart, crying for the memory of my mother.

Your grand-daughter, Amai, I thought. *A little girl at last.*

I named her Tawona, *We have seen*, as a witness to Amai's prophetic dream, and in honour of all we had suffered.

So my little girl, Tawona, grew up in the dust of my father's homestead on the reserve. I carried her on my back as I worked in the meagre fields and carried water from the river that continued to struggle, year after year. She was my constant companion. But it was hard for us, especially in the beginning.

When Tawona was born, everyone could see that her father was a *murungu*. Can you imagine what that was like? In our village, on the reserves, we were a brown people, a people of complexions ranging from ebony to coffee, to the brown of the marula fruit. Our hair was black, short, tight curls or braided, twisted with thread or tied in a *dhuku*. Nowhere amongst us had there been a child with skin the colour of a lion cub, with hair that caught the light and flamed golden, twisting in tangled curls down her back.

Tawona was at once a marvel and an oddity. When the other children were feeling generous, they played with her hair, plaiting it, plastering it with mud to make it dark like theirs. That was her favourite game. At other times, when meanness or petty jealousies mangled their games, Tawona was the scapegoat, the outsider, the one about who they would sing: *Mwana wemusango, mwana wemakwenzi.*

"Come now, children," I would say. "Play nicely!" And inside me, I cried, thinking, 'Don't you dare call her a child of the forest, a child of the bushes. It's not her fault. It was never her fault.'

Amid the difficulties of life in the reserves, Tawona was my joy. I lived for her smile. I woke up at the cock's first crow and gazed at her sleeping face, framed by bronze curls, impatient for her to wake up and caress me with her smile. I sang to her, told her the stories of Tsuro naGudo, the Hare and Baboon tales of my own childhood. I taught her the names of the trees, the flowers, the plants you could eat from, those you couldn't. I taught her how to hold a *badza*, how to plough good, straight lines, how to tend your field so that the weeds never established themselves, how to water them just enough and not too much. And, of course, I told her about Amai – her *ambuya* - who had taught me all of this and so much more. Tawona never tired of hearing about Ambuya and our home near the baobab tree.

"The baobab tree is bigger than any tree you've ever seen," I told her. "Much bigger even than Babamukuru Farai, much, much bigger!"

Her eyes grew wide at that. To her, Babamukuru Farai was the biggest, strongest man in the land. Already, he all but towered over Baba, coming to eye level with Babamunini, who seemed smaller because of his slightly slimmer build. A tree that was bigger than Babamukuru? Impossible!

"Yes, Tawona, it is bigger than your uncle. And so wide, you have to walk round and round and round before you get back to where you started. But it doesn't have branches and leaves like these trees here."

Head to one side, she asked me how come the baobab didn't have branches like these trees?

"They say that when Mwari made the earth, he threw the baobab into the earth upside down, with its roots in the air – so that's why its branches look like a tangle of roots." I drew my memory of the baobab in the mud by the river and Tawona cackled with laughter. She had never seen anything so strange-looking.

I drew her to me. "Ambuya loved that tree very much, Tawona," I said, my face in her hair. "And I was born there. One day, you will see it for yourself."

She let me hold her for a few more moments, before scrambling up to join the other children for a paddle in the water of the stream.

I sighed. One day, she would understand. My daughter would need to know her roots if she was to succeed in Rhodesia, especially now that change was in the wind, blowing in from the big cities of Salisbury and Bulawayo.

Somehow, somewhere, our people began to hold ideas that they were not taught at their sub-standard school in the townships and at the mission schools. They began to use a new vocabulary, one that did not begin and end with *yes, baas*.

They say the ideas filtered down to us from Ghana, from Kenya, from Tanzania, South Africa.

Ideas of independence, an end to oppression, equal opportunities, no more *Whites only* signs, no more Tribal Trust Lands. New names were whispered, revered, became slogans: Kwame Nkrumah, Mau-Mau, African National Congress.

Yes, there was a change on the wind. We could all feel it. It made us yearn for things we had not thought of in many years: our ancestral lands, dignity, self-respect.

It made us bold.

It was the year that Tawona started school, during the planting season. We had all gone to the fields to clear them for the new season's crop. I held a *badza* in my hand and surveyed our fields. My gaze flickered to the land, clustered with trees, that lay to the east of our allocated stretch of land. Anger bubbled in my chest. There was not enough land here to feed our family, let alone allow us to grow more food to sell in town.

"That was the whole point of the Native Land Husbandry Act," I remembered Babamunini saying. "To stop us Africans from competing with the white farmers."

But last year our family had known hunger. The rains had been poor and the earth was depleted.

We desperately needed more land, but the District Commissioner kept telling us that he was under strict orders from Salisbury not to allocate any more to individual families. I seethed. Our family would go hungry for another year because of the laws sent from Salisbury.

I went over to where Farai was standing with Baba. I took the axe from his hand and marched over the dry earth to the edge of the forest. Without a word, I lifted Farai's axe and swung it at the base of the nearest tree. The force of the blow gave me a satisfying jolt and, grimly, I raised the axe again.

"*Iwe,* Tariro, *urukuitei*?" called Baba. "What are you doing?"

But I didn't answer. I just kept swinging at the tree, the splinters striking my legs, the axe cutting deeper every time.

Farai and Mainini were the first to understand.

Wordlessly, they both took up axes and began to chop at the trees beside me. Others joined us, and soon the field was echoing with the sound of chopping axes, rustling leaves and groaning tree trunks as they began to fall.

Baba stood by and watched us for a long time. I looked over at him, wiping the sweat from my eyes.

I will never forget how he looked, the expression on his face. I saw there a mixture of anxiety, fear and, eventually, pride and understanding. If he wanted to remind us that it was against the law to clear bush for cultivation, he never did. If he wanted to remind us that we could be arrested for taking more land than we were entitled to, he never did. If he wanted to remind us that we were no longer free to do as we pleased, that this was Rhodesia, that, as *'kaffirs'*, we had to remember our place, he never did.

In the end, he simply took up an axe and began to clear trees alongside us.

It was a small thing. It was not a new political party, it was not a rally or a demonstration, it was not a representative sent to the government. But it was our way of saying enough was enough.

Later, we could blame it on that wind that blew into the countryside from the city.

16
Chimurenga

When nationalist politics reached the countryside, we Africans responded with enthusiasm. We had grown tired of accepting the white man's laws without question, of having no voice with which to argue or reason with those who made the laws.

Many communities began *freedom ploughing* as we had, asserting their voices with hoes and axes, clearing land for cultivation in defiance of the Native Land Husbandry Act. Others began to grow crops on white farmland or to destroy the contour ridges and drain strips that the government insisted on. Some slaughtered the cattle on the white farms or, as an act of defiance, refused to take their own cattle to the dipping stations.

Rippling through the countryside were feelings of revolt and unrest, feelings that were expressed by our brothers and sisters in the cities by the formation of political parties. We heard the names of some of the leaders – Ndabaningi Sithole, Herbert Chitepo, Joshua Nkomo – and our hearts swelled with pride. Even the queen of England began to talk about majority rule. Change was coming.

But then came UDI, the Unilateral Declaration of Independence. In 1965, Ian Smith declared Rhodesia independent of Great Britain – and stated categorically that there would be no majority rule in his lifetime.

When all efforts towards a peaceful settlement, negotiation, and accommodation failed, the only available route became armed struggle.

That was when young men and women began to melt into the bush, fleeing over the veld to train in Mozambique, to return as fighters in the Second Chimurenga, to set our people free. They were not alone. The spirits of Mbuya Nehanda and Sekuru Kaguvi returned to infuse the struggle with the call of destiny and ancestral approval. This was our land, the land of our ancestors. We were simply taking back what was rightfully ours.

This was what they told us, the comrades from ZANU, the Zimbabwe African National Union, when they visited our villages in the night, to hold *pungwes*, to encourage us to support them, to spy for them, to feed, clothe and warn them when the Rhodesian Forces came looking for them. And how could we not? These were our sons and daughters. We the villagers became the stream and the comrades became the fish; they melted in amongst us and, at night, they crept down through the bush to ambush Rhodesian soldiers, to place road mines in the way of army vehicles, to take revenge on white farmers who had abused their workers.

Farai went to join them.

He left with a group of comrades who had come to talk to us about the liberation struggle. I saw his eyes light up when the young man, his face obscured by a bushy beard, spoke in stirring tones about the liberation to come, about the necessity of armed resistance.

In the morning, Farai was gone.

And, in 1975, in the year Herbert Chitepo was assassinated, in the year that Robert Mugabe became the leader of ZANU, I left Tawona in Mainini's care and melted into the bush to fight alongside the comrades, our boys, *vakomana vedu*.

I see the dawn light up the sky. It has been a quiet night. No explosions, no land mines, no planes droning overhead.

I have shed tears for my brother.

I ask for the strength to be brave.

I ask for victory for the comrades.

I ask to see my daughter Tawona again.

I ask to be reunited with her in a free, independent Zimbabwe. I will hold her hand and I will take her to our baobab tree and I will show her the wide, wide trunk, and the upside-down branches. And I will tell her my birth story.

And her blue, blue eyes will light up because then she will understand who she is, and how she came to be who she is.

And she will understand why I left her behind, why I fight, why I pray that I survive this war so that I can share the fruits of independence with her. Fruits that, unlike the fruit of the baobab, will be sweet, so sweet that all the bitterness will be forgotten.

PART 2

Katie

Zimbabwe 2000

17
A farmer's girl

I was a farmer's girl through and through. I grew up on a farm just outside Masvingo, amid the dust, the heat, the ebb and flow of the seasons, the sounds of the night: our dogs barking, mosquitoes whining, the throb of cricket song.

Before I turned fourteen, my world was small, relatively untouched by outside forces. I never watched the news or read the newspaper. As far as I was concerned, political parties and elections, Economic Structural Adjustment, AIDS, war in the Congo, had nothing to do with me. I could understand why Patience, the maid, listened to Radio Two while she worked. She needed to know all those things. Those were her people – blacks – in the news. As for me, my people – white Zimbabweans – were hardly ever on local radio or TV.

Our world was different from theirs. Our world

revolved around our farms, our hundreds of hectares where we grew cotton, tobacco, oranges, tea, to bring in foreign currency and to fund overseas holidays.

Most of us had houses in the low-density suburbs, complete with pool, tennis court and *braai*, serviced by quiet, obedient blacks; we had sports clubs where we played and watched cricket, hockey and rugby and where the old folks played bowls; we went to schools where the best traditions of the English public school were kept alive with blazers, boaters and three-stripes-if-you're-late, where our own history was celebrated through House names like Rhodes, Selous, Livingstone and Moffat, and school songs that praised the pioneering spirit of our predecessors; our parents drank in bars where UDI memorabilia decked the walls and where you could still laugh at a *kaffir boetie* – a white person who loved blacks – without fear of reprisals.

As a white farmer's girl, I lived a charmed life that revolved around my family and school. My concerns were personal and private – my relationship with my father, my feelings towards my mother, the twins. There were no climactic events, no major catastrophes, no insufferable losses – just the muted angst of a white, middle-class family, a family of farmers dealing with the business of living.

That all changed in the year I turned fourteen.

In the days before I was sent off to school, back in those days that now seem faded, like an old photograph, I roamed our farm, wild and free. Mom never knew where I was because she stayed indoors or, at most, in the fenced-off flower garden. Grace, my nanny, tried to keep an eye on me but I always managed to shake her off. I wanted to explore, to find new places to play, new anthills to crunch under my feet, new beetles to catch, to stain my hands, feet and face purple with mulberries. And to find Dad.

Dad had started farming as a young man, after a stint in the Rhodesian colonial administration, and now he spent his days overseeing the work on the farm - grazing, herding, branding, dipping. We were cattle ranchers; the land wouldn't support anything else.

I can see Dad now: well over fifty, but still tall and sturdy, in his khaki shorts and *veldskoens*, his beloved bush shoes. He is standing out in the hot sun, shouting orders to the farm workers, his skin burnt and freckled, his bush hat pushed back on his head, creases at the corners of his blue, blue eyes from squinting into the sky, looking for signs of rain.

I had always loved my father, more than I could ever tell him, more than he would ever know. Even though he could be impatient and curt – and was known as a 'no-nonsense *baas*' by our workers – he was always gentle with me.

Whenever he saw me walking towards him, winding my way through the long, dry grass in my bare feet, his face broke into a smile.

"Katie!" he cried, reaching out to me. "How's my big girl?"

I laughed and ran into his arms, never mind the prickly grass and the clinging blackjacks. He swept me up and put me on his shoulders and we went walking. That was how I got to know the land: from high up on my father's shoulders.

We walked like that for hours, sometimes in silence, other times chattering about everything and anything. We talked about the animals, the farm, what we would like for lunch, which bird was calling, which tree was snapping its pods, spraying its seeds.

Usually our walk ended under the big baobab tree, next to its enormous, wide trunk, under its sprawl of bare branches that reached out above us like a tangle of roots. *The upside-down tree*, I called it.

We would sit there and rest, hot, sweaty, panting for the water that Mom had sent with Dad, frozen in the deep freeze the night before.

We drank slowly, not all at once, cooling down. In that hot, close air, all we could hear was the lazy buzzing of the flies, the *kree-kree-kree* of the grasshoppers and the distant lowing of the cows.

Those were the sounds of my childhood, the symphony that accompanied me every day until I had to be trussed up in a checked dress, blazer, my broad, barefoot feet stuffed into shoes that were still tight with newness, and driven off the farm to the nearest school. I cried that first day, not because the teacher was strict or because the other children teased me about my freckles. I cried because I couldn't go walking with my father any more.

But that was a long time ago. I had long since got used to the routine of school, hymns sung with gusto in the mornings, swapping sandwiches at lunch-time, times tables and hockey in the afternoons in winter, swimming in the summer. My school was full of other farmers' children like me and, together, we carved out a niche for ourselves, secure in the knowledge that, when we went home, we had hundreds of hectares to lose ourselves in, horses to ride, house girls and garden boys to fetch and carry and spit 'n' polish our shoes.

I started boarding school in Form One. My boarding school, the old, esteemed St Paul's College, was on the other side of the country, hundreds of kilometres from home. But it was the best there was and Mom wasn't going to settle for less than the best schooling for me.

"Besides, Ian," she had said when they were discussing the issue of my schooling with Auntie Janie and Uncle Mannie, "it's one of the few schools that has managed to hold on to its white teachers. All the farming families send their kids there…"

"Those who can afford it," added Auntie Janie helpfully.

Uncle Mannie, he of the gold cuff-links and silver Mercedes Benz, clinked the ice in his glass of single-malt whisky and smiled smoothly at Dad. "If it's money that's the problem, old chap, I'm sure we can come to some arrangement…"

At that, Dad flushed a deep red and glared at Uncle Mannie. "It's not a question of the money, Mannie," he replied. "Thank God we've nothing to worry about there. I'm just not sure that a boarding school that far from home is the right thing for Katie."

"But all the schools around you are full of blacks, man!" interjected Auntie Janie. "That can't be what you want! Just look at the state of them: all their white teachers have left, the black teachers don't know what they're doing and everything has gone to the dogs. Believe me, you're better off sending her further away where she still stands a chance of getting a decent education, like the one we got in the old days."

That decided it, and a few weeks later we drove up to St Paul's College, set in acre upon acre of rolling green fields where, on one side of the road, the boys played rugby and cricket, fostering school spirit by shaking the skies with their mighty war cry.

On the other side of the road, at the girls' school, imposing colonial buildings stood in the shade of mauve-tipped jacaranda trees, the reception walls adorned with the prize-winning work of the 'A' Level Art students.

"I'm sure your daughter will feel right at home here," explained the headmistress in the nasal, clipped accent of all town-bred, well-educated whites. "We look after all our girls – and we are proud to say that many farming families trust us with their daughters' education and have done for years now."

Mom and Dad enrolled me on the spot.

18
Rudo

St Paul's College was an amazing experience for me. Aside from the demanding curriculum, there was an extensive range of sports and club activities to choose from. Teachers provided instruction and tuition in subjects as diverse as photography and sewing skills, astronomy and ballet, choir, public speaking and individual music tuition for those learning an instrument.

In time, I overcame my shyness and discovered that I had a talent for singing. I was soon committed to choir practice twice a week, as well as extra voice lessons with Miss Vorster. She was preparing me for the annual Eisteddfod competition, to be held in Harare later in the year. We were working on 'I dreamed a dream', from *Les Miserables,* Mom's favourite musical.

But there were other learning experiences too. For the first time in my life, I had to share close personal space with black children.

Surprisingly, there were quite a lot of black girls at the school. I hadn't expected that. I suppose I thought they would not be able to afford it – or would have preferred to go to school with their own, just like we did.

"Well," Mom explained, "some of the blacks are very wealthy, you know, especially the ones in the government. They want the best for their children, just like we do, and they know that they can get that at schools like St Paul's. But you just stick to your own, my girl, you hear? They may be able to afford the same school as you and all that, but they're still *munts* at the end of the day. They're not your equals."

So, it was with some trepidation that I saw that my nearest room-mate was a black girl from my class, a girl called Rudo.

Rudo was the same age as me and she too performed in the school choir. Her voice was a strong alto and she had an amazing ear for harmony. With her neat, braided hair and coffee-coloured skin, her private-school accent and insatiable appetite for Jane Austen and other classics from the library, she seemed a world away from the blacks back home.

She didn't smell like them, for a start. I had

thought that all blacks smelled the same: a mixture of dust, sweat, cooking oil and Lifebuoy soap. But Rudo smelled of bubblegum lip-ice and the same deodorant Mom used. She didn't eat with her hands or pronounce her 'l's as 'r's. She was not what Mom and Dad would call a *'munt'* at all.

And Rudo didn't treat me like other blacks had all my life: like a little 'madam'. She didn't speak to me in the deferential way that the blacks on the farm did. She spoke to me quite normally, as if it was the most natural thing in the world for a black girl and a white girl to be friends. On the very first day, she came right up to me and introduced herself. To my surprise, she asked me about my family, about our farm, whether I had a boyfriend. I blushed then, and mumbled my replies, but she just laughed and sauntered off to the library.

I later found out that her father was a government minister and that her family owned a lot of land in the Eastern Highlands. Her father had attended St Paul's before independence when it was one of the few private schools to allow blacks to enroll. He was an Old Boy and extremely well connected.

"He was one of the first black Rhodes scholars," Rudo told me proudly. "And he's got a degree from

Oxford – talk about a tough act to follow, eh?"

I nodded mutely, still trying to take it all in. Neither of *my* parents had been to university, let alone Oxford. They had no black friends or colleagues, just the workers on the farm. As far as I knew, none of the books on our bookshelves had been written by or about blacks. Nothing worthy of respect, nothing that mattered, had been achieved by blacks. That was one of the unalterable truths I had grown up with.

Rudo was the first person to make me start questioning those truths.

She laughed at me later on that night too, when I was washing my *broekies* in the sink. "Hey, man," she said. "I thought it was only us blacks that washed our underwear at night!"

"No," I replied, defensive. "My nanny taught me to wash them myself every night. I've been doing it since I was nine."

"Cool, hey," she remarked drily.

I plucked up the courage to say more. "What, d'you think we not clean or something?" I had never considered that perhaps others didn't see us as we saw ourselves.

"Well," she said, her head to one side, "you Rhodies are not exactly known for your culture and breeding… and everyone knows that white girls don't like to wash – they use perfume instead!"

"That's not true!" I protested hotly. "That's really unfair. You don't know anything about us." But even to my own ears, I could hear how hypocritical I sounded.

So that was how Rudo and I became friends. But I always held back, just a little. I knew how Mom and Dad would feel about me getting chummy with a black girl.

It was the April school holidays and everyone in the school was going home. We had all packed our bags, exchanged addresses and shed our tears. Now we were waiting for our parents, relatives and guardians to come and collect us and take us home, to Harare, Bulawayo, Mozambique, Zambia, even far-away Tanzania.

Rudo and I were talking about what we planned to do over the holidays.

"Well, I plan on catching up with all my friends from primary school. We haven't seen each other in *ages*, man! My friend Shingai said she's going to have a party this holiday, her first proper party, with DJs and everything!"

"Really?" My eyes were wide. "That should be great, *lekker*! My aunt Janie has invited me to spend a week with her at her house in Borrowdale."

"Hmm, Borrowdale Village?" enthused Rudo. "The shopping's wicked there."

"Yeah, I know, hey!" I said, grinning. "A whole week of swimming, sunbathing, playing tennis, and checking out Harare's finest..."

"Oi!" Rudo slapped my arm. "Don't go forgetting about my brother! You know he has the hots for you! He keeps asking about you, you know..."

"*Ja*, hey," I said, pulling a face. "As if!" I couldn't help an involuntary shudder as I pictured her brother, Max, star of the St Paul's rugby team, head of the debating society – but as black as coal. A black boy? No way.

"Well, anyway," Rudo said, "I can't wait to finally meet your parents! And Luke and Jessie! You've told me so much about them, I feel like I know them already!"

Just at that moment, Mom and Dad entered the hall, Luke and Jessie holding their hands, scanning the crowd for their big sister. As soon as they saw me, their faces lit up and they ran towards me, calling my name.

I went forward to meet them and, in a moment, we were hugging, and I was laughing at the news that tripped off their tongues, about the farm, the horses, school, and the ginger cake that Patience had baked in honour of my homecoming. Mom and Dad began to walk towards us, smiling.

I heard Rudo call my name and I saw Mom craning to see who I had been sitting with. I saw her eyebrows rise and her nostrils flare, ever so slightly. My eyes flicked to Dad's frowning face, a question in his eyes.

I knew exactly what was wrong.

And I knew exactly what I had to do.

"Mom! Dad!" I said, smiling broadly, hugging them, taking them by the arm and steering them away from where I had been sitting. "What took you guys so long?" We began to walk towards the entrance.

"Who was that black girl calling you, Katie?" asked Mom.

"Oh, just a girl from my class."

As we reached the entrance, I turned back to see Rudo sitting there, stunned, as if she had been slapped in the face. I gave her a little wave.

She didn't wave back.

19
Home again

The heady scent of gardenias reached me from the flower beds that lined the visitors' car park. It was a gorgeous April day. The rains had been good and the lawns, hedges and flower beds around the school were lush and green. The dew from the early morning had long since dried as the sun rose confidently into mid-morning.

Dad took my bags and threw them in the back of the *bakkie*, our truck. Then Luke, Jessie and I clambered up, giddy with familiar excitement and, with every moment, I felt myself shedding my private schoolgirl persona and becoming a farm girl again. It felt good.

I hardly gave a thought to what had just happened with Rudo. As far as I was concerned, there was no other way I could have handled it – I knew the rules, even if she didn't.

"You look so smart in your uniform, hey," said

Jessie, fingering the thick fabric of my blazer.

"Thanks, Jessie," I smiled, ruffling her hair. "And you just keep getting cuter every time I see you!" I hugged her again, hard.

"What about me, Katie?" Luke hated being left out. "Am I big and tough like Dad? Am I?"

"Of course you are! Come here, let me feel those muscles!" And he clenched his little fist and let me marvel at the size of his miniature biceps.

"You know Sheba had pups, Katie? Wait till you see them, man, they so cute!"

Sheba had been my dog forever. We had eight other dogs, ranging in size and breed from a tiny, wiry Fox terrier to a great, loping Great Dane. But Sheba, the Cocker spaniel, was my special pet, covering my blankets with her hairs, chewing my books and filling my room with her dog smell. I loved her to distraction and couldn't wait to see her puppies. A rush of happiness flooded through me. I was going home and it was the holidays – what could be better, man?

As we drove home we chatted, the countryside whizzing past on either side of us, the hot wind whipping our hair into knots and tangles that would be cried over in the shower later.

We stopped at a lay-by under a huge baobab tree. I looked up at the thick, thick trunk that rose into the sky above us, the spread of branches right at the very top. Like a giant, sticking his enormous hand right out of the earth to claw at the heavens.

"Hey, Dad," I said, "how's our baobab at home? She's at least as big as this one, isn't she?"

"Ja, definitely," was Dad's reply. "Ours is maybe twice the size of this one."

There was a connection between us: the baobab, Dad and me. Back in the days before I started going to school, and even afterwards, our farm walks would often end under the baobab tree. And Dad would talk to me about it.

"120,000 litres!" he would say, his hand on the tree's great, swollen trunk. "That's how much water one of these can hold!"

It was Dad who told me that the baobab could grow to be over 25 metres high, that many of them were thousands of years old. I would look up in awe, wondering what this tree must have seen in all that time.

Mom didn't share our interest in the baobab, or the

rest of the flora and fauna of the farm for that matter.

"*Ag, sies,* man," she would say in disgust, "that has to be the ugliest tree on God's green earth! That thing is like all these native trees: ugly! I mean, look at this place!" And her slim arms would sweep out to either side of her body, her bracelets jangling, her red nails like sweeps of blood in the air, marking the stone mountains, the golden veld grass, and the flame lilies that I loved. "If it wasn't for our imported trees and flowers, this place would be Hell on earth!"

Dad wouldn't say anything, of course. He never did when she spoke like that. He would wait quietly for her to finish her rant, scratching the back of his neck, making sympathetic sounds. This was Mom's time now.

Because whenever Dad and I came back in from the world we shared, I faded into the background and had to be content with looking on at the drama unfolding between my father and my mother. Twenty years his junior, Mom had stolen Dad's heart and it had not been long before Dad had divorced his first wife and married Mom, an act that some members of the family still found hard to forgive. I was the result of their obsession with each other – or rather, Dad's obsession with Mom.

Dad loved Mom, totally and unquestioningly. He lived for the times that she sat, her feet in his lap, talking, laughing, teasing. The way he looked at her, it was as if he couldn't believe that something so beautiful, so glamorous, was actually his.

But Mom? Mom was beautiful but thorny, just like a rose. She was hard to read, difficult to predict. The smallest thing could set her off, and then there was nothing to do but wait until her mood subsided. Of course, Dad knew how to bring her round but I resented the way he pandered to her every whim, as if she was all that mattered to him.

She had wanted a closed veranda, so she got it. She had wanted a pool and she got it, even though it cost a fortune to run and water was scarce enough already. She had wanted an enclosed garden with a lawn, green grass and carefully tended flower beds, and the garden boy struggled to give it to her, even though the land fought him at every turn.

But, as far as Dad was concerned, no price was too high to pay for Mom's smile.

So, as I grew up, I became used to seeing him pay that price, over and over and over again.

By the time we got home, it was time for lunch on the veranda.

"Patience!" Mom screeched. "Where's the tea, man? What's taking so bloody long?" Then her voice dropped to a low mumble as she passed round the bread, the cold chicken, butter, the salad of thin-sliced tomatoes. "That's the trouble with these bloody people, hey, they just don't listen…"

'These bloody people'. That's how Mom referred to the blacks who worked for us. Sunday, the cook, Patience, the maid and Grace, my nanny. We had a gardener too, who looked after Mom's kitchen garden but she only ever called him 'the garden boy' when she spoke about him. I heard Grace call him Lovemore, but I don't think Mom knew what his real name was.

But once Mom had her tea, she was better. Then she sighed and sat back in her chair, her feet up in Dad's lap, and started to talk normally. She asked me how things were going at school, when I would be performing with the choir.

"I told Auntie Janie all about your Eisteddfod and she is so excited! She said she'll definitely be there."

"That'll be great, Mom."

"Ja, it will, won't it?" Then she turned to Dad, her eyes bright. "I was thinking, Ian, that we could make a weekend of it. Why don't we all go down to Harare, visit some friends, take the kids to the Village? They've got a great flea market on Sundays! We could go see a play at Reps, go out to eat…?"

Dad smiled and said nothing.

"Oh, come on, Ian!" Mom cajoled, her hand on his arm. "It'll be *fun*!"

Dad patted her hand and smiled again. "You go, babe, you go with the girls. Luke and I, we've plenty of work to do here on the farm. You go and enjoy yourself."

Dad knew that she would. That was her world, not his. She was a city girl and she loved city things. She was quite good about being stuck on the farm, though, most of the time. Like, she would ask Dad how things were with the *mombies*, the cattle, and he would always say that things were '*lekker*, hey'. He never gave too much detail because he knew that she wasn't really that interested – it was just something to talk about.

After lunch, Luke and Jessie ran off to ride their bikes down the dirt track that led to the stables. "Come and see the horses, Katie!" they called. "Come and ride with us!"

"I'm coming now-now," I called back. "Let me

finish my lunch." I reached for a mango, my thumb caressing the tiny bumps on the otherwise smooth, red-tinged skin. My mouth watered at the thought of the firm, sweet flesh inside, the juices that ran down your wrist, yellow-sticky, the ropy strands that got stuck between your teeth if you got a really ripe one.

Mom and Dad pushed their plates away and lit cigarettes. Blue-grey flames danced lazily in front of Patience as she cleared away their dishes.

"We'll have coffee now, Patience," said Mom.

"Yes, Madam," Patience replied softly. Then she looked up at me. "Welcome back, Madam," she said, smiling shyly.

I smiled back. "Thanks, Patience," I said. " It's great to be home...." Then I stopped. This was Patience, not Rudo. Mom and Dad had always been very strict on the correct way to behave with servants.

"You must always let them know who's boss, Katie," Mom would say. "Don't get chummy or they will try to mess you around."

"That's right," Dad would add. "These people only respect you if you're strict with them. I learned that when I used to work in administration in the rural areas. They'd only respect you once you had shown them who was boss. So don't ever make the mistake of treating them like they're your equal. They never will be. White is white and black is black. It's as simple as that."

Now Dad's voice was grim, as he looked out towards the pool. "I got another letter today," he said. "A letter about the farm. This time, they're saying we have ninety days' notice to leave."

Mom put down her cup of coffee with a clatter. "No, Ian!" she exclaimed, her face suddenly pale. "No!"

"What's all this, Dad?" I had heard nothing while at school.

"The government has been saying for some time that it's going to redistribute farm land. Now they have started writing to some farmers, telling them that they have to leave, that their land is going to be given to blacks." His lip curled and his blue eyes flashed. "They claim that the land is rightfully theirs, that it was stolen during the colonial era..."

"Oh, give me a break, Ian!" exclaimed Mom. "As if this government cares about all that! They just want to get their hands on more land so that they can keep lining their pockets! Honestly, these bloody people..."

"You know, just yesterday, my boy Frank

discovered that some of these so-called 'war veterans' have been hanging around, asking the farm hands what kind of *baas* I am, whether I treat them fairly."

"Bloody troublemakers," said Mom.

"I won't have that nonsense around here, Sue, I'm telling you. My boys know: they step out of line, they get the whip, simple. And a couple of ex-terrorists hanging around isn't going to change that."

I had seen Dad beat one of the farm hands before. He had caught him stealing and decided to handle the matter himself rather than get the police involved, as he often did. He had beaten him with the *sjambok* until the boy's back was a mass of black and red stripes. I could still hear the sickening whistle of the whip flying through the air before it bit into the flesh.

Dad continued. "I won't end up like that poor chap they killed last week. He let them get away with too much. The bastards came and took over his place, drove him off and shot him... and the government hasn't done a bloody thing about it."

I shivered. Someone had been killed?

All of a sudden, a breeze blew in from the garden, upsetting a precariously balanced china milk jug, sending it sliding off the table to smash, in many milk-white shards, on the sun-baked concrete floor.

The milk began to dry immediately.

"Patience!" Mom cried, her voice edged with panic. "Come here! Come and clean this up!"

But I knew that the hysterical undertone had nothing to do with spilt milk.

20
Mom

Dad didn't speak about the dead farmer again but it played on all of our minds. I couldn't help feeling that another of the unalterable truths I had grown up with was being unravelled: the idea that we whites were safe, secure, untouchable, that things would remain as they were.

After lunch, I went to my room, my sense of foreboding stilled, at least for the moment, by the discovery that everything was as it had been the last time I was there. I felt again the thrill of the familiar creak on the living room door, the worn, woven carpet in the corridor, Gran's watercolour paintings still on the walls.

My room was as I had left it: Patience had kept it spotlessly clean, and I sighed with pleasure at the sight of my lavender patchwork quilt, my dolls lined up on a shelf, my book and butterfly collection waiting to be updated.

"Katie!" I heard Mom calling me from her room.

I expected to find her pale and anxious but, instead, I saw that she had reapplied her lipstick and was smiling at me. I realised, with a jolt, that I had almost forgotten how stunning she was.

"I got you an outfit to wear to the *braai* this weekend – do you like it?"

It was from one of the new boutiques in Harare. It spoke of style and sophistication – but wasn't too grown-up. Of course I liked it.

Mom and I were as different as a rose and a flame lily. Mom was beautiful, almost too beautiful. I remember being aware of her beauty – and how important it was to her – from a very young age. Perhaps it was the way she spent long, luxurious minutes cleansing, toning and moisturising her skin with an array of lotions that smelled like garden flowers and lavender. The way she rubbed thick, glossy cream into her hands, hands that never knew blisters, massaging her cuticles until her nails shone, pink and perfect.

The way she held her head just so when I clambered up to hug her – 'Mind my hair, Katie!'

I used to sit on her bed, my scabby, tomboy knees drawn up to my freckled chin and gaze at her, watching her transform her already lovely face into something altogether more arresting, more alluring. The smoky eyes with the impossibly long eyelashes, the smooth, peachy skin, glowing with blusher, the crimson-red lips that she stretched over her pearly teeth as she painted them, rubbing them together before slicking on another layer.

Sometimes, she would spray me with some of her perfume, and I would close my eyes as the tiny fragrant droplets caressed me, like fine rain, enveloping me in a haze of glamour and beauty – I wasn't me any more, not knock-kneed, tomboy, freckle-faced, redhead Katie. I was Mom.

That was when I would try on all her pairs of high-heeled shoes, one by one, tottering along the corridor, draped in an evening gown that dipped down at the back and fell right off my thin shoulders, the long skirt slithering like a snake of sequins along the parquet flooring.

Mom would be gentle then, generous. A touch of powder, some eye shadow, a bit of lipstick never hurt anyone. And then I was Mommy's little girl, cast in her image.

But it never lasted for long. Sooner or later I would stumble in her shoes, damaging the heel, the floor, or my ankles, tripping over her dress, shedding sequins. Then she would frown and tell me to 'take all that stuff off, man'.

And I would run outside to be Daddy's girl again.

<<<<<<<<<<<<<<<<<<<<<<<<

That first day home was a lazy one. I went down to the stables with Luke and Jessie, and got reacquainted with the horses, stroking their strong flanks, enjoying the feel of their velvet-soft noses, their whispering lips as they picked carrots from my hand.

Afterwards we went for a dip in the pool and, when we were puckered like prunes and our eyes stung from the chlorine, we came inside and had hot showers. Then Grace took Luke and Jessie to have their supper in the kitchen and Patience came to Mom's room with tea and cake.

That afternoon in Mom's room stayed with me. If I close my eyes, I am there again: the late afternoon sunlight dappling through her lace curtains, playing shadows on the walls and on her white linen bedspread, like a thousand cobwebs; the chorus of birdsong, shrill, from the garden; tthe dogs barking outside the kitchen door; the maid calling to the gardener to bring more onions from the garden; the rich, comforting smell of chicken stew that rose up from the kitchen. All so clear to me, like yesterday.

Mom and I talked, our voices rising and falling, weaving in and out of each other in the golden light of late afternoon. I had a look at her latest South African fashion magazines, she asked about who had said or done what at school, caught me up on all the family gossip, asked if I needed a new bra yet.

Then we painted each other's toenails – I did hers first. Carefully, I rolled up shredded pieces of cotton wool, just as she had taught me, and pushed them between her toes so that they splayed out, like little starfish. She chose a colour, a pretty coral pink, and I shook the bottle, unscrewed the cap and, tongue between teeth, stroked the tiny brush from the cuticle to the end of the nail, taking care not to leave any gaps. Just as Mom had taught me. Then she painted mine, a pearly colour, a gift from Rudo.

I think I remember that day so vividly because that was the last time things felt normal. Because, after that day, nothing felt normal ever again.

21
Independence weekend

The next day was Zimbabwe's Independence Day. Everyone was off school, off work, to celebrate 20 years of independence. At Heroes' Acre, under the red, green, gold and black flag, there would be ceremony and speeches commemorating the so-called 'fallen heroes' of the Second Chimurenga, what Mom and Dad still referred to as 'the bush war'. The fiery speeches, songs and fist-pumping – '*Pamberi ne*ZANU!' – would be broadcast on TV, after the eight o'clock news. We never watched it though. It was something for the blacks. It was their celebration, something to rub in the whites' faces: *we won, you lost*.

Even the colours of the flag were a rejection: green for the land, gold for the wealth, red for the blood spilt while fighting for freedom, equal opportunity and majority rule, and black, well, black for the people, of course. After all we had done to make the country what it was when they took over, no mention of us whites, even though there was white on the flag. No mention of us at all. Not our flag. Not our war. Not our country.

Not any more.

Mom was in high school during Rhodesia's dying days. Her own brother, my uncle Ralph, died fighting for the Rhodesian Security Forces in 1974. Like practically all whites, aside from those people Dad referred to as '*kaffir*-loving liberals', our family had been fiercely against rule by the black majority. My family had supported Prime Minister Ian Smith when he unilaterally declared Rhodesia independent from the UK in 1965.

Several family members, my grandfather and uncles included, actually volunteered to fight in the Rhodesian Security Forces. They didn't need the call-up or propaganda posters – 'Rhodesia needs YOU' – to persuade them. Even Gran did her bit for the war effort, volunteering to man a radio station that connected the farms in her area to the security forces, in case of a terrorist attack.

"As far as we were concerned," Dad told me, "we were fighting communist terrorists, protecting ourselves and our way of life. There's no shame in that."

Mom didn't like talking about that time – it brought back too many memories for her. Only on the anniversary of Uncle Ralph's death, after a few glasses of sherry, did she allow herself to remember. "He died a hero," she would sniff at last, wiping away tears, blotting the pools of mascara. "He died fighting for what he believed in."

But there would be no ceremonies at Heroes' Acre for Uncle Ralph.

On those days, the whole family would reminisce, telling booze-soaked stories, opening the wounds of the past, making us younger ones listen – 'lest we forget'. It was horrible. They talked about the radio reports of atrocities committed by the terrorists – ears and lips cut off, fed to the victims, white families like ours, massacred. How they had to travel in an armed convoy whenever they left town, how they had all, from five-year-old kids to senior citizens, learned how to clean and load an old 303 rifle.

"We whites had a lot to lose," Dad explained. "Rhodesia was home to us. We had already told the British to get lost in 1965 and we were proud to be called Rhodesians, to have this amazing place to call our own. We were never going to let her go to the dogs like all those other so-called independent African countries – I mean, look at what happened to them!"

He was talking about all the other African countries that had been ruled by whites – British, French, Portuguese – but had, by diplomacy or guns, taken charge of their own affairs and declared themselves independent: Ghana, Kenya, Mozambique, Zambia, Malawi, and others.

"We were surrounded by them," said Mom. "We were the final frontier, holding out against the whole world – the most civilised country in Africa, apart from South Africa, of course. I mean, they tried everything: threats, sanctions, you name it. But we stood strong. We Rhodesians weren't going to go down without a fight." She never tried to hide the pride in her voice.

So I did find it confusing when, in our history books, the whites were portrayed as the invading colonisers, the settlers who stole the land and oppressed the black majority: the villains.

Needless to say, our family never tuned in to watch the blacks celebrating our defeat at Heroes' Acre, but because it was a public holiday, we often had a huge family *braai* at one of our farms. That year, the year I turned fourteen, it was Uncle Paul's turn to host the clan at the family's tobacco plantation.

That Saturday morning, the pink-tinged silence of dawn was broken by Captain, our strident bantam cockerel, crowing at the top of his voice. I stumbled out of bed, tripping over Sheba, my Cocker spaniel, who was still snoring away, far away in dog dreamland. Luke had been right: her puppies were just the cutest things and, as soon as I came home, I moved them all to my room.

From downstairs, the aroma of coffee wafted towards me from the kitchen. Patience, the maid, was already there and, by the smell of things, she had been busy.

When I went into the kitchen, I saw that Patience had already packed some freshly baked bread, a roast chicken, mangoes, guavas and a huge bunch of finger-small bananas in a big picnic basket. On the table were various containers – coleslaw, chicken drumsticks, pasta salad. There was a crate of drinks on the floor. Our contribution to the *braai* menu. Patience had also baked a Victoria sponge for Gran – Gran always asked for her Victoria sponge every time we saw her.

She was putting the cake into a sturdy plastic container when I came in. She looked up at me and said, "Good morning, Madam."

"Morning," I said curtly, remembering my slip-up the day before.

But Patience didn't seem to notice. She didn't even have her customary smile. She looked as if she had hardly slept.

Tentatively, wary of seeming too friendly, I asked, "Everything all right, Patience?"

Patience looked down and pursed her lips, concentrating on fitting the lid of the plastic container. Two tears dropped on to the checked tablecloth.

I just stood there, one hand on the handle of the fridge door, the other slack at my side. I didn't know what to say, where to look. I had never seen any of the servants cry before. I really didn't know what I was supposed to do.

More tears dropped and Patience wiped them away and sighed deeply, her hand on her chest, looking down.

After standing there, mute, for several moments, I couldn't stand it. "Don't cry, man," I said, trying to sound reassuring. "Don't cry. What is it? Has something happened?"

At that moment, Patience burst into a flood of tears and sat down abruptly at the table, covering her face with her apron. Through the hiccups, I could just about hear what she was saying. "Ah, Madam," she sobbed, "my brother, he is dying. He is very sick. They say he only has a short time to live… no cure… pneumonia… haven't seen him… must go…" Her words became increasingly inaudible until she collapsed in a bout of sobbing.

That was when Mom walked in. Her eyes widened when she saw the scene in front of her: the maid wailing into her apron over Gran's Victoria sponge.

"Patience!" she said sharply. "What's going on here?"

At the sound of Mom's voice, Patience stood up immediately and tried to control her sobbing, twisting her hands in her apron, her eyes on the floor. She knew, as I did, that the madam didn't like this type of thing.

"Nothing, Madam," she whispered, her voice hoarse.

"Don't be stupid, girl! I can see that there's something wrong, now what the bloody hell is it? Another family emergency?"

Hesitantly, Patience told Mom about her dying brother in town, about how he only had a short time left and how the whole family had requested that she come as soon as possible.

Mom listened, a frown on her face, her thin arms folded in front of her. When Patience had finished, Mom let out an irritated sigh.

"Oh, Patience, this really is very inconvenient. I need you here to keep an eye on things! If I let you go, who will make sure the garden boy feeds the dogs and doesn't steal from the kitchen?"

Patience timidly suggested that Frank, our farm manager, come to watch the house and keep an eye on the garden boy. "That one is very strong, Madam. You don't have to worry."

"Oh, all right then. Make sure you're back on Sunday. I will have the boss tell Frank to come and keep an eye on that boy, to make sure he doesn't take anything from the kitchen."

Patience smiled, grateful, thanking Mom again and again.

"All right, all right," Mom said gruffly, "that's enough of that. But no pay for this time off, OK? You bloody people are always having some family crisis or other."

Patience's smile dropped, ever so slightly, and she blinked a few times before nodding and hurriedly returning to the business of getting our breakfast on the table.

Mom stamped out of the kitchen. She was always in a foul mood until she had her morning coffee and cigarette. When she got upstairs, I heard her telling Dad about what had happened downstairs, her voice high with complaint.

"Probably dying of AIDS, like the rest of them," I heard Dad say.

And then I felt bad for Patience, really bad. We had learned about AIDS at school. I could just picture Patience's brother, skin and bone, his thin, baby hair rust-red, wasting away. The teacher had said something like one in four Zimbabweans had HIV. They were dropping like flies.

I was glad that Patience had managed to get time off to go and see her dying brother, even if she could only stay for a day and would have to forfeit part of her wages.

21
On the road

Mid-morning saw Patience on her way to Harare on the bus, having cleared the kitchen and explained to Frank, Dad's manager, exactly what needed to be done. I saw him saunter up to the kitchen door, tall and lanky, his huge fists swinging at his sides. The garden boy trotted behind him, eyeing him warily.

I had noticed that Frank was not very popular with the other workers – they spoke to him as little as possible and, when they did, it was formal, nothing like the easy banter they used amongst each other. Frank had been Dad's farm manager for about 10 years and he trusted him more than anyone else on the farm. Frank was always keen to carry out any punishment my father decided on – threats, beatings or dismissal. The garden boy was right to be worried and he quickly got to work boiling up bones and mealie-meal for the dogs' midday meal.

My aunt and uncle lived more than 100 kilometres away. Their farm was at the end of a long stretch of road that cut through granite *kopjes*, small, rocky hills, studded with native huts, before running through broad stretches of grassland, fenced in on either side.

On the way, we passed groups of black women with babies tied to their backs and improbably large loads on their heads, making their way to selling points along the main road. There, they would unpack their bags and lay out the fruits of their labours – baskets, wall hangings, pottery, jewellery – to sell to passing tourists.

We arrived at Uncle Paul's tobacco farm at two in the afternoon.

Dad looked out of the window as he drove up the old road leading to the farm, beaming at the lush, green leaves that waved in the breeze, row after row after row. He pushed his bush hat back to run his fingers through his hair. Coming home always energised him. Perhaps it was the great fields of tobacco that seemed to roll on, endlessly, whispering of a good harvest and continued prosperity. A trip to South Africa, maybe even to England or Australia to see family. A new *bakkie* to drive, an investment on a holiday cottage, an A-class boarding-school place for another child. All these were possible with a good harvest.

Soon we reached the driveway and Dad hooted twice. As we drove up the long drive, the dogs bounded out to greet us, running alongside the car, barking, tongues lolling.

At the end of the drive, I could see the white walls and steep, thatched roof of the farmhouse. Way back, before UDI, Grandad had designed it in Cape Dutch style with a central front door, shuttered windows to either side, and a beautiful gable, curved and elegant, rising up from the centre of the thatched roof. On either side of the front door, Gran had trained roses to grow over a wrought-iron frame and bursts of bougainvillea – purple, white, vermillion – framed the façade of the building.

I had always loved that house. It was gracious and hospitable, always open to family and friends, Gran made sure of that. For me, it symbolised the permanence of our family, who we were. I was so glad when Uncle Paul moved in, when Gran and Grandad grew too old to manage on their own. I wanted that house, and the land around it, to stay in our family always.

In fact, all of that land – Grandad's tobacco fields, Gran's spice-scented kitchen garden, the shady, green orchard and the great bush, teeming with wildlife, beyond it - held a special place in my heart: I had so many memories there.

Behind the house, beyond the gum trees, lay the lake where all my cousins and I had once swum while it rained, braving sheet lightning, bilharzia and the fish that nibbled at our toes. In the shade of the banana tree grove was the orchard where Gran used to grow the oranges for her legendary bitter marmalade and where my young cousins and I gorged ourselves on hard, green mangoes, fuzzy loquats and pink-fleshed guavas. My first pony, Biddy, a lovely, sweet-natured bay, was born in the stables to the east of the big house.

Coming to my grandparents' house, the homestead that drew our family together from as far afield as South Africa, Zambia and Great Britain, didn't feel like visiting. It felt like coming home.

22
Family reunion

Everyone was there by the time we drove up to the homestead. We could see their cars lined up along the driveway: Uncle Paul's *bakkies*, two of his own and one each for his eldest boys, Auntie Bernadette's Hilux, and Auntie Monica and Uncle Marius' Landcruiser with its South African number plates.

Uncle Paul, tall and burly with a beard grizzled with grey, still rugged in his shorts and bush hat, was standing in front of the rose bushes, his hands on his hips, his glasses reflecting the glare of the sunlight, hiding his blue eyes, so similar to Dad's. He watched us drive up to park under the lush trees that shaded the other cars.

As we stopped the car, I saw Auntie Bernadette emerging from the house. Her floral dress was crisp in the sunlight, flapping in the breeze. She stepped to Uncle Paul's side and took his arm, looking over at us, a sunny smile on her face.

We all got out of the car, stretching our cramped legs, breathing in the heady scent of Gran's roses mingled with the dust-dry smell of the bush and the salty-smoky smell of roasting meat from the *braaivleis*.

"What took you guys so long?" Uncle Paul's voice always sounded muffled by his bushy beard. "We've had the *braai* going for two hours, man!"

Dad strode up to his brother and they shook hands, their faces open, smiling. It had been a while since they had seen each other, Gran and Grandad's golden wedding anniversary party, in fact. Dad leaned over and kissed Auntie Bernadette on the cheek.

She smiled up at him, pursing her lips. "Nice to see you again, Ian." Then she turned to Mom, who had just walked up from the car, holding Luke and Jessie by the hand. Auntie Bernadette narrowed her eyes and looked Mom up and down, fleetingly, before cocking her head to one side, like a secretary bird.

"Sue…" she cooed, her voice tipped with ice. "You're looking… well." Secretary birds are well known for their strength and vigilance, and their ability to dispatch pests in a deadly and decisive manner. Auntie Bernadette was no different.

Mom looked back at her and said evenly, "And you, Bernadette, and you." A perfunctory kiss in the air inches away from Auntie Bernadette's ear and Mom was free to greet Uncle Paul who gave her a decidedly warmer reception.

Auntie Bernadette recovered and managed to compliment the twins and give me a hug without missing a beat. "Let's go inside," she suggested. "Mom and Pop have been waiting for you guys."

We stepped into the living room, which was dark and mottled after the blinding white light from outside. The sunlight was filtered through lace, framed by heavy muslin curtains, handmade by Auntie Bernadette. The old moss-green sofa was strewn with crocheted cushion covers bought from the local women's co-operative. The wall shelves were cluttered with family photographs.

There was a plastic dome - the kind that makes snow if you shake it - that Grandad had brought back with him from his one trip to London. It stood on the mantelpiece, next to the cups and trophies, shields and medals that Dad and his brothers, and Uncle

Paul's sons, had won for rugby, cricket and swimming during their years at boarding school. Then there was Grandad's framed collection of colonial photographs showing dignified white settlers, trussed up in top hats and crinolines, posing with half-naked natives, hung on the walls.

I had always been embarrassed by those pictures. I wasn't sure what made me more uncomfortable: the dark, gleaming skin on the topless women and men in loincloths, or their vacant expressions.

"They're like children, Katie, remember that," Grandad said. "These blacks really don't have much going on upstairs, hey. That's just the way they are."

Grandad was sitting in a chair by the lace-curtained window, smoking a pipe, reading a farming magazine. He looked up when we came in and his face broke into a smile. "Well, well, you finally made it!" His voice was rough with years of smoking but his delight was unmistakable. "Well, what're you waiting for, you little scallywags, come and give your old grandfather a hug!"

Luke and Jessie ran forward and threw themselves on him. Being fourteen, I was a little more reserved but I grinned when Grandad said, "Growing lovelier every time I see you, eh, Katie? Isn't she, June?"

Gran appeared behind us, her arms out. "Of course she is, Peter!" She laughed as she looked up at me, giving me a hug. "And getting taller all the time too!"

As soon as we had greeted Auntie Monica, Dad's younger sister, her husband, Uncle Marius, and their two gorgeous daughters, Angie and Nicola, Gran insisted on taking all the little ones to see the baby animals and pick strawberries for dessert.

Auntie Monica, who was expecting again and looked tired and puffy, offered to go with them. Auntie Bernadette left to supervise the girl in the kitchen and Uncle Paul rounded up Dad, Uncle Marius and Mom for the customary tour to see how things were going on the farm.

"Come on, you guys," he said, turning towards the open front door. "I want to show you a sample of the latest crop before we eat. Katie, you can go and join the others out by the pool."

Mom pulled a face at me as I gave her a cheeky grin. Neither of us was that keen on tobacco plants but it seemed that I, at least, had managed to escape the obligatory walking tour this time round.

The pool had been built by Uncle Paul when he took over the running of the farm. Auntie Bernadette had insisted on it – she didn't like the idea of her only daughter, Elaine, swimming in the lake with her brothers and their friends. As it happened, once the pool was built, it became the favoured hang-out for Elaine's brothers and their teenage friends.

Not that she should have worried about Elaine. Ever since I had known her, my cousin Elaine had been painfully shy, uncomfortable with the height she had inherited from her father, aware that her gentle ways and compliant nature made her a perpetual victim in this house dominated by dogs, boys and guns. Even at the age of twenty-two, she still stuck out like a sore thumb.

Outside, I found her sitting on a deck chair with Shane's fiancée, Jane, seemingly engrossed in a book but with a face that was flushed deep red.

"Hi there, Elaine," I said, sitting down next to her.

"Oh, hi, Katie," she answered in her quiet voice. She only looked up at me for a moment before returning to her book.

"Hi, Jane."

Jane pushed her face into a smile as she glanced at me. "Hi, Katie," she chirped. "So nice to see you again." And then she turned her adoring gaze back to Shane.

Elaine's brothers, Neil, Shane and Christopher, strong, strapping lads with a passion for beer and rugby, were all sitting in and around the pool, drinking beers out of brown bottles.

Unlike my cousins on Mom's side, many of whom were my age, I had never really developed a relationship with Uncle Paul's boys; the age gap between us had always been too wide. My only memory of time spent with them was of that daredevil swim in the lake when I was eight. And last year, of course. I shivered and rubbed at the goosebumps that rippled over my arms, each hair erect with disgust and my secret shame. I forced myself to look over at the boys again. They were laughing about something, something to do with Elaine.

"Remember his face when he saw Dad giving it to that *munt*, Shane?" spluttered Neil, wiping the back of his hand over his lips.

"*Jislaak*, he almost kakked himself, man!" hooted Shane, tears running down his sunburned face.

"Hey, Elaine!" called Christopher, looking over at his sister. "What made you bring old Lover Boy out here, anyway? Didn't you know that he wouldn't be able to hack it?"

Elaine bit her lip and stared at the pages of her book. Long experience had taught her that saying anything would only result in more teasing, more laughter at her expense. So she kept quiet.

But that didn't stop them.

"He looked like a bloody *moffie*, man, in his dress pants and fancy shirt. I nearly died laughing when he actually gave Mom a bunch of flowers – what a loser!" They all spat out some choice names for Elaine's visitor, names so crude even I was blushing. Jane tittered prettily, her eyes flickering nervously between Shane and Elaine.

Abruptly, Elaine got up and walked off into the house. "See you later, Katie," she whispered, tears edging her voice like lace.

"Hey, Katie!" Christopher, the youngest of the boys, waved his bottle at me. "You want a beer?"

I took a deep breath. "Na, hey, not now." Mom would absolutely kill me if she caught me drinking. I wasn't about to risk that.

They all looked at each other and burst out laughing. Even I had to admit that I had sounded ridiculous and my face flamed again. I wanted to go inside, to find Elaine.

But Christopher was still talking to me.

"So, how's St Paul's treating you?" Christopher was in his final year at the boys' school. I had seen him play on the school rugby team and we had exchanged brief words.

"It's all right," I said, shading my eyes from the sun. I could feel all their eyes on me and I felt suddenly uncomfortable.

Christopher drained his bottle, then tossed it on to the grass before loping over to the ice-filled basin by the outdoor bar to grab two more. He passed the table where I was sitting and put the brown bottle in front of me. "There you go," he smirked. "Just in case you change your mind..." Then he sauntered back to the poolside and lowered himself into the water, his arms hooked up on the concrete side, watching me intently.

Suddenly he spoke again. "You know what?" he said. "A really funny thing happened on the last day of term."

"What's that, Chris?" asked Neil, rolling his head towards his brother.

"There's this *munt*, right, on our rugby team, Max, a real uppity chap, hey, thinks he's white, some minister's son or something." The other two nodded as Christopher warmed to his theme. "Well, anyway, one day after a game, I hear him talking about this white chick that he's got the hots for." And he was looking directly at me when he said it. My blood ran cold.

"*Ag, sies,* man!" spat Shane. "That's disgusting!"

"Oi, he had the hots for a white chick?" gasped Neil. "He must be a really cheeky one, hey! You guys are slacking, man, how'd you let him get so cheeky? That would *never* have happened in my day!"

Christopher laughed and took another drink, his eyes burning, never leaving my face. "*Ja,* man, *ja*! That's when I realised that we'd been too soft on these buggers. So, on the last day of school, we sorted him out good and proper, me and the other boys. Gave him something to take home for the holidays ..."

"You mean you gave him a bloody good hiding, eh?" The other two roared with laughter and clapped Chris on the back.

My mouth felt like I had been sucking on baobab tree fruit – so dry I couldn't swallow, let alone speak.

Max.

Rudo's brother.

Oh my God.

I felt a sense of powerlessness, of despair, seep

through me. All of a sudden, I knew why Christopher had been looking at me like that. A white girl with a black boy was the ultimate taboo.

The conversation drifted elsewhere and then Shane was calling Jane to join them in the pool. She refused, said she didn't want to have to change her clothes. But Shane laughed and, with the agility of a leopard, jumped up out of the pool, a blur of muscle and water, and ran over to grab her. She realised, a split second too late, what he intended to do and, screaming, tried to run away. But she was too slow and, in moments, Shane had her in his arms, pinned against him.

She was laughing at first, scolding him. Then, when he didn't let go, she started shrieking as he half-dragged her over the brown-tipped grass to the edge of the pool. Jane began to cry, as she struggled to free herself. But I was the only one who saw this. The other boys were falling about, laughing, and cheering Shane on.

With a twist of his body, Shane hooked an arm under Jane's kicking legs and, hoisting her into the air, he pushed her out, out, out over the lazy green water.

She fell as if in slow motion, her eyes wide, her hair streaming. Then the splash that wet the sides of the pool and drove the dogs crazy, their bodies wagging along with their tails as they barked and ran from one end of the pool to the other.

It was a few moments before Jane emerged, spluttering, thrashing at the water, and Shane was there. She screamed at him, pounding at his bare chest with her small fists, as he held on to her, still laughing. Then he kissed her hard, right on her screaming mouth, and she was quiet at last, and the boys hooted and clapped: the perfect finale.

I was embarrassed and looked away, but a shadow passed over me and there was Chris in front of me, dripping wet in his Speedos, his face alight with a crooked smile, his eyes burning into mine. He reached out for the bottle in front of me and said, in a conspiratorial voice, "Funny, hey, that *munt* kept going on and on about this girl, this girl called Katie. But I thought to myself, 'no way, not my Katie, no way.' Right?"

And I felt my bowels shift as I remembered what he had tried to do to me in his room last year, when I was thirteen. He had said he wanted to show me his CD collection. But I didn't remember anything other than how his breath had smelled of cigarettes and smoked beef in the suddenly dark room, his hands hot and rough from farm chores, still clutching a warm bottle of beer.

I looked away then, but he put his finger to my chin and turned my face towards him.

"Don't worry," he said softly. "It'll be our little secret, OK?" He winked and smiled again before throwing his head back and taking a long drink of beer.

I was glad that Mom and Dad appeared just then on the veranda.

23
Family secrets

The maids – under Auntie Bernadette's expert guidance – had laid out a fantastic spread. The meal was wonderful: the bitter taste of what had happened earlier fading with every greasy lick of the lips and every sip of fragrant peach juice, all the way from the valleys of the Cape.

Hands moved over the table, the oldest to youngest and back again, passing plates, bowls, reaching for glasses, pouring from bottles that stood in the ice bucket. At first, everyone was too hungry to speak, so eager to taste the spicy kick of the meat that had been marinating since the day before – as it always did – and was now infused with the smokiness from being grilled on the open coals of the *braaivleis*.

After ice-cream, cake and a glorious fruit salad, Auntie Monica's girls, Luke and Jessie dragged me on to the lawn where I chased them around with the water hose, totally drenching them, one by one, while they shrieked and squealed with delight. They ducked and dived, pulling each other towards the bushes, trying to wrestle the hose from me while I, an artist with the rubber tube, alternated between rolling ropes of water, stinging jets and a rainbow-crowned spray, all with a flick of my thumb. We had a great time.

When at last they ran off to climb the smooth-limbed guava trees, I went back into the house to change my clothes. Grandad and Gran had retired to the living room. The late afternoon heat was too much for Grandad. Outside, I could hear my older cousins splashing in the pool, the dogs barking, loud laughter from the men on the garden chairs. But I didn't feel like putting on my swimming costume and going out there, not with the way Christopher had been looking at me all afternoon. Inside was safer.

I walked over to the mantelpiece. I looked through the cards from various family members, congratulating my grandparents on their golden wedding anniversary a few months earlier. I picked them up, one by one, comparing the designs, reading the messages, enjoying the feel of the creamy cards, admiring the silver, embossed lettering.

Then I came across a card that was different from

the rest. This one wasn't displayed upright, like the others. It was lying face-down on the far end of the mantelpiece. And it looked different too. Instead of the usual rings, bells and silver sprinkles, this card was made of a rough, handmade paper with what looked like leaves and wild flowers pressed into it. In the centre of card, there was a montage made up of a guinea-fowl feather, some cowrie shells and two black-and-cream, striped porcupine quills. I had seen handmade cards like this in the fancy stationery shop in Borrowdale, on our last visit to Harare. I opened it to read the message inside. It read simply, 'Thinking of you with love on your special day. J'.

'J'. Who was 'J'? And why didn't this 'J' sign his or her name properly, like everyone else?

Just then, Dad came up behind me. I could smell the whisky on his breath when he said, "Hey, Katie, what's that you've got there?"

He reached over my shoulder and picked the card out from between my fingers. Briefly, his blue eyes scanned the queer collage on the card's cover, then the writing on the inside. His face went red and he curled his lip before turning to Gran.

"James sent this to you?" he demanded, shaking the card at her. Gran's face went pale and she glanced at Grandad to see if he had heard. But he was asleep now, his head low on his chest, snoring lightly.

"Shhh," shushed Gran, motioning for Dad to put the card down, to put it out of sight. "It's nothing, Ian, just a card! Nothing more…"

"Just a card?" Dad's eyes blazed but he stopped waving the card and walked over to Gran, behind Grandad, so that he would not see him. "Just a card? So, have you spoken to him too? Has he called you?" Without waiting for a reply, he began to pace up and down the room. "You should have sent the damn thing back! The cheek of it!"

Then I understood what all the fuss was about.

'J' was my disgraced uncle, James.

I remembered so clearly the last time I saw him. I was nine years old. It was my Auntie Monica's wedding. Uncle James, young, handsome, funny Uncle James, had pitched up with a goatee beard and a black woman on his arm.

I remembered the shocked glances, the whispers, the titters, and Uncle James, striding through the garden between the tables with the white tablecloths and rose centrepieces, as bold as can be, holding this black woman's hand, not caring that everyone was staring at him.

Auntie Monica screamed at him later, blamed him for upstaging her and ruining her wedding day.

"You always were selfish and pig-headed!" she screamed. "I never want to see you again, I hate you!" She had left the reception in tears and it was left to Dad and Uncle Paul to tell Uncle James that, until he came to his senses and stopped making 'a bloody fool of himself', he was not to show his face again.

But Uncle James was defiant: he told them to stop living in the past, that this was not Rhodesia, this was Zimbabwe and they'd better get used to it.

That was when Dad punched him.

Uncle Paul looked at Uncle James leaning against the wall, holding a handkerchief over his bleeding nose, and said, "You make me sick, you know that?"

Later I heard Mom and Dad talking as they got ready for bed. Dad was still livid and I could hear the champagne from the wedding party slurring his words, tipping his anger to boiling point. "Who the bloody hell does he think he is, Sue? Eh? Just tell me that!"

Mom tried to soothe him. "Oh, he's just young, Ian, young and rebellious. It's just a phase he's going through, you'll see…"

"No, this isn't a phase, Sue, he's always been

like that: a *kaffir*-loving fool! I'm telling you, there's something wrong with that boy. Always cosying up to the blacks, getting involved in politics, filling his head with rubbish! He was like that at school, you know! Couldn't turn your back without him going off to talk to some bloody *munt* or other – he even learnt the language, for God's sake! He's a disgrace, he is! A bloody disgrace!"

That was when I put my head under the blankets and shut out the sound of Dad's loud voice, ugly and hard with a hatred that I wasn't used to, not towards family, not towards one of our own.

And I felt bad because I really liked Uncle James. He had always been kind to me and he was the one who taught me how to swim, in the shallows of Lake Kyle, the year before when he was still welcome on family trips. So I closed my eyes tight and prayed that Uncle James would come to his senses and be allowed back into the family again – I missed him.

But then he had gone and married that black woman and ruined any chance he might have had of being forgiven and let back in. Of course, none of us went to the wedding, although I saw the invitation when it came, and saw Dad curl his lip and tear it into little pieces.

At the time, I had been horrified. I couldn't understand how he could stoop so low – to marry a black woman? Someone like Grace or Patience? It didn't seem right, it *wasn't* right! It went against everything I had ever known about the proper way that black and white should relate to each other. But then I met Rudo – and I began to think that maybe it wasn't as bad as I thought, as bad as everyone thought. But I didn't say anything, ever. Like most of us, I hadn't seen or spoken to my Uncle James in five years.

But now it seemed he had re-established contact, sending Gran and Grandad a card for their anniversary. Well, if the card was anything to go by, he wasn't quite ready to come back and play the role of the prodigal son.

I wondered how many times he had written to Gran, secretly, maybe sending photos. He had always been her favourite and I could see, from the way Gran was talking to Dad, that if her youngest son had reached out to her, she wouldn't have pushed him away. Gran wasn't like that. So I wondered…

24
Fighting talk

Soon it was time for sundowners: drinks, smokes and conversation that did not involve women and children. Gran, Mom, my aunts and younger cousins were all watching a movie inside, seeking refuge from the mosquitoes.

I sat curled up next to Dad, unnoticed, sleep tugging at my eyelids. I felt myself drifting into that space halfway between dreams and consciousness and I let myself float, float… but the men's voices kept pulling me back.

"So," began Uncle Marius, settling himself in his seat, "what's Uncle Bob been getting up to, eh? I heard he's been getting a bit hot under the collar lately."

'Bob' was Robert Mugabe, Zimbabwe's president since 1980.

Uncle Paul frowned. "He's started mouthing off about land, man, getting the blacks excited about it all over again."

"Could get a bit tough for you chaps, hey? You know how emotional these blacks get about land. Looks like old Bob's chosen the right cause..."

"Bloody opportunist, that's all he is, that Mugabe," muttered Dad through clenched teeth. "Never gave a damn about redistributing the land until those bloody war veterans started making a fuss! Now this is his ticket, his way of playing the war hero again – and staying in power!"

"That's not strictly true, though, is it?"began Uncle Marius. "They've always had their eye on the land - just couldn't get too many folks to sell up, before."

"Well," announced Grandad, his voice slow and tremulous but heavy with conviction, "I've said it before and I'll say it again. We're not going anywhere. This is our land. My father first farmed here over 100 years ago, then I established the farms that Paul now runs. Soon, young Shane here will be ready to take over. That's four generations of investment and hard work! They can say what they want but this is our family's land, and we have the title deeds and everything to prove it. We helped build this country – they have no right to kick us out."

My heart thudded in my chest, as loud and

insistent as a thousand horses' hooves. A dry, tight pain constricted my throat when I thought about what they were all saying: could the blacks really get rid of us, just like that? Could we really lose our farm, our land, our *home*?

"Well, Pops, I'm afraid it might not be that simple. They're saying that those deeds aren't valid because, according to them, the land was stolen…"

"Stolen? We bought that land, fair and square! I paid £2,000 for 400,000 acres, in cash! Cecil Rhodes had a treaty, he had a charter. Everything was above board – and they know that!"

Uncle Marius snorted. "Well, if you call £2,000 for 400,000 acres 'fair and square'..." But he trailed off when he saw the angry flash in Dad's eyes.

"Anyway," added my cousin Shane, "what do you think will happen if they try to touch us, if they try to kick us whites off the land? Then they'll really be in for the high jump. All those multi-national companies, the foreign investors, will pull their money out of here before you can say 'liability'. They would be crazy to risk it…"

"Ag, Shane, you don't know Bob," Dad muttered grimly. "He *is* crazy. And if he thinks that going after us will keep him in power, you better believe he's going to do it."

Shane was unconvinced. "But surely the British government won't stand by and let that happen..."

Grandad spluttered, his face purple with rage. "The British?" he spat. "They're the ones responsible for this mess, the bloody lot of them. They're the ones who kept pushing for blacks to vote, and then they sold us out and gave the country over to those Communist thugs! The British? Don't make me laugh! A bunch of hypocritical cowards, that's what they are! We could have won that war, you know!"

At that, Uncle Paul's sons, Neil and Shane, groaned. "Ag, Grandad, not that again!"

"You pipsqueaks better listen to your elders and betters!" barked Dad. "Your grandfather is right. The Rhodesian Army was never defeated in that bush war. We were betrayed by the British and by some lousy two-faced Africans. We had better weapons, better training, better..."

"Ag, man, Ian, spare us the tales of your military successes!" Uncle Marius laughed. "Look, I'm just glad that no one in South Africa is talking land redistribution. Your blacks are quite a peaceful lot – apart from those crazy Ndebeles, of course – but ours? They a savage bunch, man, especially those Zulus!

Those guys will kill you dead in broad daylight, just to steal your trainers! Just think if they started going after the white farmers in South Africa..." He shook his head and muttered a curse before draining his glass.

"Marius, you've got a bloody nerve saying that," said Dad, "what with you cosying up to the blacks in that government of yours in South Africa! I mean, how the hell do you sleep at night, knowing that you're working for those terrorists, Mandela, Mbeki and the rest of the ANC, those African National Congress guys?"

"Very well, actually," replied Uncle Marius smoothly, looking up at Dad. "Firstly, there were killers on both sides. Don't think for a moment that our police and army guys didn't do their fair share of that. What do you think the State of Emergency was all about? But aside from that, you have to remember that I am not a farmer, I am a businessman. I'm a *realist*. I do business. And I will do business with the next man, be he white, black, Indian or Coloured. I will work with whoever is in power to protect my interests – and those of my family."

Then Uncle Paul, who had been glowering into the coals of the *braai*, burst out, "It's bloody nonsense, man, all of it! They haven't got a hope in hell of running this place without us. Without our expertise, our management, our investment, this place would go to the dogs like the rest of Africa. The blacks are incompetent, man, anyone can see that. Just compare the country today to how it was during UDI or before 1980 – it was a paradise, man! Then they had to come and spoil it! Well, we won't let them ruin what we have taken years to build, that's for damn sure!"

He would have carried on if Auntie Bernadette had not come lumbering out of the back door, her eyes wide with fear, her face haggard in the light of the fire.

"Paul!" she shrieked. "Come! Come quick and see the news! Oh my God, Paul, oh my God! They found that farmer who went missing! It's started, Paul! *It's started*!"

There wasn't enough room for everyone around the television. No way near enough for the staring eyes, the mouths open in horror, the hearts thumping with a new, unfamiliar fear. But there was just enough room for us all to catch a glimpse of the bloodied face of a white man, one of us, a cattle rancher, shot dead, and the blacks, the 'war vets', singing and dancing in their orange overalls, beating their war drums, triumphant, celebrating the take-over of the farm.

Celebrating the start of the Third Chimurenga on the 20th anniversary of Zimbabwe's independence.

25
Bloodshed

Panic sang in the air like a million mosquitoes. It only took half an hour for everyone to get ready to leave, exchanging words of encouragement – 'This will blow over, man, it has to.' But although bravado tripped off the tongues of the men, the women's eyes betrayed the fear we all felt. Auntie Bernadette was crying, hiccuping sobs that shook her huge frame, her eyes red-raw and swollen. She had known the farmer they had found dead. His wife was a fellow volunteer at the hospice, his children had stayed at their house, swimming and fishing in the lake.

"Those poor boys," she kept saying. "Those poor things." Then she buried her face in Uncle Paul's checked shirt and sobbed again. "How could they do this, the animals?"

Uncle Paul was silent, his face stony behind his

glasses. I could see that, as far as he was concerned, now was the time of men, of men with iron will and courage. His whole life had prepared him for this time. He had lived through it before and was ready to live through it again.

Shane tried his best to reassure Jane, who was teetering on the brink of hysteria. Uncle Paul told him to get her a drink or give her a slap. Her hands shook as she gulped the drink Shane held for her.

Immediately after watching the news report, Uncle Paul went to his study and came out with three guns – two rifles and a semi-automatic – and handed a rifle and a torch to Shane.

"Go to the servants' quarters, Shane, and call Petros and Innocent. Get them here now, I don't care if they sleeping or whatever."

Shane nodded gravely, whistled for one of the dogs and left the house through the kitchen door.

Once he was gone, Uncle Paul looked around at us all. "Right, people, I think we'd better call it a night. Ian and Sue have a long way to go – and we don't know what kind of evil is out there tonight."

Gran spoke then: "Let's say a prayer for their safe journey and for God's protection in this time."

We all joined hands and Grandad led us in a short

prayer. Mom squeezed my hand so hard I thought the bones would crack. Then I saw that her eyes were squeezed shut just as hard and her shoulders were shaking. It almost made me more afraid than the sight of that white man on the television screen, his face blotched with blood, his eyes rolled back in his head.

After the prayer, Auntie Bernadette turned to Mom and gave her a hug, enveloping Mom's slight frame in the folds of her floral dress. "We all in this together," she murmured. "Drive safely and call us when you get home."

Mom blew her nose and nodded gratefully. "We will, I promise."

The kitchen door banged and Shane came in with the dog, its tail wagging, energised by the unexpected night walk.

"Innocent and Petros are waiting outside the kitchen, Dad," reported Shane. His young face was flushed with new responsibility, with the promise of proven manhood.

Uncle Paul nodded and strode out of the living room. I was standing near to the kitchen and I slipped inside to watch the exchange between Uncle Paul and two of his oldest servants.

The porch light showed Uncle Paul standing with

his hands on his hips, his legs planted apart. The two older black men in front of him looked as if they had been dragged out of their beds. Their heads were bowed and they only glanced at Uncle Paul's face fleetingly.

"I want to know whether you have seen anyone strange around here," began Uncle Paul. "There's been some trouble with a white *baas* not too far from here, bad, bad trouble. Do you boys know anything about that?"

The two men glanced at each other, their brows furrowed, their hands behind their backs, and then they shook their heads vigorously.

"No, *baas*, we don't know about any trouble," quavered Petros, cowering slightly, his two hands cupped together in front of him, as if he was pleading with Uncle Paul to believe him.

Uncle Paul looked at the two men for a moment, then said, "Right, well, there's been some trouble so I want you to keep a look out for anyone strange, anyone who doesn't work here, and bring them to me. Tomorrow, you will go down the farm workers' quarters and check if anyone has been there or is staying there. If there is, bring them to me. Security has to be tight around here from now on, d'you understand?"

The two men nodded.

Uncle Paul turned to go, then remembered something. "Oh, and you know those squatters down by the riverbank? The ones that arrived a few weeks ago?"

"Yes, baas…"

"Round up their cows, dig up those crops of theirs and set fire to those disgusting shacks. It's about time we had some law and order around here." With that, he turned on his heel and strode past me, back into the living room where everyone was ready to go.

Uncle Paul came and shook Dad's hand feelingly. "Drive safely, man," he said, "and get that place of yours secure quick-time. We don't know what these crazies will do next so it's best to be prepared."

Dad nodded. "Sure, Paul, we'll call you later. Look after Mom and Dad, OK?"

"Ja, will do."

Then we were out of the door, into the moonlit night, the sound of over-excited frogs throbbing in the night air.

But that night the darkness felt menacing, full of secrets, as if we were being watched. All we knew was that we had to get home, get back to our land, get back to the guards, the guns, the dogs that would rip a man's throat out at the sound of a whistle.

The ride home was long and tense. No one spoke. Luke and Jessie fell asleep, too young to make sense of the images on the television, of the new threat that hung, low and brooding, over our lives.

I couldn't sleep, although my eyes were raw from watching the road appear in front of the headlights. At any moment, I expected us to hit a cow or a buck, for a car tyre to burst, anything to stop us arriving safely. But up above us, the moon sailed through a placid sky, studded with stars, as if nothing out of the ordinary had happened. I said silent prayers as I huddled next to Mom, who had fallen asleep with her head against the car window. I could see the tear stains on her cheeks.

After what seemed like forever, I recognised the turn-off to our farm. There, reflected in the car's lights, was the rusting old sign which announced that Baobab Ranch was one kilometre down the dirt track.

My heart soared to see the bend in the road that came just before the driveway to the house – but happiness soon gave way to concern. I couldn't see the porch lights twinkling through the long grass, winking at me, telling me that the house was still there, that we had made it home safely, that everything was fine.

Everything wasn't fine. Not at all.

"Eh?" Dad's voice was thick with incomprehension. "What's going on here?"

For a start, the dogs were running around outside in the driveway, circling each other, baying. It was an unearthly sound, the kind of sound they usually made when they went hunting for game with Dad and smelled blood. The sound sent a chill licking down my spine and I saw Dad's hands clench the steering wheel.

He put his foot on the accelerator. "What the bloody hell is going on here?" he muttered, craning his neck to try to see beyond the car's lights, trying to avoid hitting the potholes and the maddened dogs.

"Dad…" I wanted him to slow down, sensing danger. But he didn't. "Dad!" I said, louder this time. "Slow down, Dad, the dogs… you might…"

Then I felt a bump and heard an anguished yelp. My heart lurched as Dad slammed on the brakes. One of the dogs?

"Bloody hell!" he muttered and opened his door,

only to be besieged by a writhing mass of dogs' paws, tongues and barks. I was faster than him. In seconds, I had clambered over Mom and was out of the car, running round to the side I had heard the sound coming from.

The car lights were still on and I could see her clearly, lying with her head on the ground, her leg bent at an unnatural angle, her fur dark and matted with blood.

"Sheba!" I cried and flung myself down beside her, cradling her head in my hands, my tears dropping on her dark, sticky fur. The whites of her eyes shone in the moonlight and she whimpered softly.

Dad appeared above us, his flashlight shining down on Sheba's leg. He whistled softly. "Jeez, Katie," he whispered, "I'm so sorry…"

I choked back my tears and bent over Sheba's quivering body. Fury flooded through every part of me, every vein, every artery, souring my blood.

Where was Frank? And that garden boy? Why had he let the dogs out? Why hadn't he looked after them like he was supposed to? My anger and hurt had me up in a moment, charging past Dad, running towards the house where I could see the sleeping body of a tall, black man on the *stoep* – it was Frank.

I began yelling before I got close to him. "Wake up!" I shrieked. "Wake up, man! What are you doing sleeping? Why did you let the dogs out? What were you thinking? Now Sheba's been run over – and it's all your fault, you stupid, irresponsible...!" Words spilled out of my mouth, faster than I could think.

I expected Frank to wake up, shocked and startled, rubbing his eyes and trying to look like he hadn't really been sleeping.

But instead he groaned and slowly turned his face towards me. I screamed when I saw it, screamed and screamed and screamed. The silver moon lit up the gash on his forehead, his mouth, wet and red and gaping with missing teeth, his eyes bruised and swollen shut, his breath coming in short bursts, bubbling as if under water.

Dad came running over to hold me as I continued to scream, hiding my face in my hands, trying to block out the sight of the man's face, pulsing with pain. Dad held me hard against him, steadying me, looking over at the man who writhed in agony on our front porch.

"Jeez..." Dad breathed. "We'd better get him to hospital..."

Mom came running up but let out a stifled cry, put her hand to her mouth and turned away, as soon as she saw the blood. Dad steered me over to where she was standing and she put her arms out to me.

"Mom," I whispered, my eyes searching hers. "Sheba..?"

Mom bit her lip and shook her head. "I'm so sorry, Katie…"

But I didn't hear any more.

Darkness covered me over like a thick blanket, muffling all sound, dulling all feeling, easing all pain.

I wanted to stay in the darkness forever.

26
The dark is rising

I didn't get out of bed for a long time the next day. Each time I felt myself rising closer to consciousness, surfacing, the sounds of the house and garden becoming clearer, I willed myself back into the abyss. I drifted in and out of dreams, dreams in slow motion about china splintering, spilling milk, the shards cutting a black man's face to ribbons, Sheba lapping up the spilt milk until she fell into a deep sleep, her fur dark and sticky, her puppies circling her, mewling, searching for milk.

I woke crying every time.

Mom came in and put a hand on my clammy forehead. I kept my eyes shut. She sniffed, and pulled her shawl closer around her shoulders.

"Mom," I said. "Where are Sheba's puppies?"

"I told Patience to take the basket of puppies downstairs. Dad said he would deal with them."

She came again, some time later, with some toast and tea. I told her I wasn't hungry.

"But you have to eat something, darling," she said, her brow furrowed, her eyes red with tears. "You need to build up your strength."

I sighed and propped myself up against my pillows. I could feel the back of my head start to throb and my eyes stung with the threat of tears.

"Oh, Mom!" I cried. "I can't believe Sheba's gone!" And I buried my face in her shoulder.

"I know, love," she crooned, "I know."

The thought of that bruised and bloodied face came back in pieces at first, each piece slipping into place so that the horror of last night was suddenly clear before my eyes.

"What happened to the boy, Mom?" I asked, my voice quavering. "What happened to Frank?"

"Oh…" Mom flushed. "Your dad drove him to the hospital, he's still there…"

"Up you get, Katie, there's no time for feeling sorry for yourself." It was Dad, tall and dark in the doorway.

"Ian," pleaded Mom, "she's been through a lot! Sheba meant so much to her – let alone finding the boy bleeding on the porch…"

"And she'll go through a helluva lot more if she doesn't get up and sort herself out." And he knelt down at the side of my bed. "Come on, Katie," he urged, his voice as I remembered it as a little girl, his blue eyes searching mine. "Where's my brave girl, eh? I want to show you something."

I got up and, in twenty minutes, I was downstairs, drinking a strong cup of tea, smiling bravely at the fraught faces of the twins, greeting the dogs.

I had to make it through the day, the best I could.

‹‹‹‹‹‹‹‹‹‹‹‹‹‹‹‹‹‹‹‹‹

Dad took us out that day. We all piled into the *bakkie* and went bumping down the farm roads, past the cattle pens, the dipping station where all the local Africans also brought their cattle to be dipped, the stables, then the wide expanse of dry-gold grasses that waved in the breeze, pasture for the cows.

We all got out of the truck then, the sun hanging low in the impossibly wide sky above. On this side of the farm, only thorny acacias dared to challenge the sky's clean, unbroken lines. The grass swished and swayed to the song of a thousand crickets and we walked there, Mom, Dad, Luke, Jessie and I.

We walked right through it, waist deep, inhaling the smell of hot, baked earth, of dust, of the *vlei*.

Far behind us lay all that we had built: the rambling house with its flagstones and wide windows, the honeysuckle and jasmine that hung over the sprawling veranda, the guest houses, the workers' compound, the dam, the borehole, the sewage system.

"Look at all this, kids," said Dad, his voice breaking. "This is what it's all about. A man's got to be able to stand tall on his own land, the fruits of his blood, sweat and tears. This is what we've worked so hard for. Don't you ever forget that, you hear?"

This is where I belong, I thought, *this is my home.*

We returned to the *bakkie* in a dream-like state, lulled by the afternoon heat, by the steady jolting of the truck, by the birds that dipped and soared in the purple-pink sky. We drove towards the baobab tree.

That was when we saw them.

The squatters.

They came out of their makeshift shelters to look at us, their clothes scruffy, the women carrying babies on their backs, their chins tilted defiantly.

Dad's hands gripped the steering wheel as he swore under his breath. Mom pressed her lips together and said nothing.

"Who are those people, Daddy?" asked Jessie. "I don't like the way they looking at us."

"I'll be damned if I know," muttered Dad, stopping the car. He jumped down from the *bakkie* and strode towards the group of people gathered in front of their shelters.

Dad raised his voice, as he always did when talking to blacks: "You guys shouldn't be here! This is private property, d'you understand? You have to take your things and go, or there will be trouble!"

A tall man stepped forward, slowly, confidently, although he walked with a limp. He wore orange overalls and a bush hat and he peered at Dad through his glasses. "You are the boss on this farm, isn't it?" I thought his tone was provocative, not at all respectful as I would have expected.

Dad drew himself up to his full height. "Yes," he replied. "Yes, I am the owner of this farm."

The man chuckled. "Yes, your workers told us all about you..." He turned to the men and women that stood around him. "Comrades, what did our brothers and sisters say about this man here?"

They all began talking at once, in a mixture of Shona and English:

"He beats his workers..."

"Unfair dismissal…"

"Low wages…"

"Won't employ trade union members…"

"Racist…"

Dad's face went red with rage and he snatched the hat off his head and pointed a menacing finger at them all. "You're the bloody trouble-makers that have been stirring things up round here! Well, I'm not going to stand for it, d'you hear? You picked the wrong farmer to mess with! You get off my land or else…"

"Your land?" The man repeated, looking around at the others, who were shaking their heads, looking over at us in the *bakkie*. "Your people *stole* this land! This is not *your* land. It is now time for justice to be served…"

"Oh, for crying out loud!" Dad shouted. "Why can't you people move on? What's done is done, man, can't you just..."

But the man cut Dad off, his eyes blazing. "What's done is done?" he said. "Is that the best you can do? Let me tell you something. My comrades and I fought for this country's independence; we sacrificed our lives, our youth, and our futures, for this country. And what have we received in return? Ha? Nothing but empty promises and betrayals."

"Well, that's something you should discuss with your president. I haven't agreed to sell anything and the government agreed to a 'willing seller, willing buyer' policy. You don't have a leg to stand on."

The man smiled then, a triumphant smile that made my insides turn cold. "The times are changing, man. The days of protecting your privileges at the expense of the majority are at an end. Try calling the police to deal with us. Try calling the army. I think you will find that they are more interested in ensuring that you comply with your order to vacate. It was ninety days, wasn't it?" And with that, he turned around and stalked off into the nearest hut. The others all melted away, looking balefully back at us.

Dad swore again and slammed the door of the *bakkie*.

Mom began to cry.

Luke, Jessie and I sat silently in the truck, a strange sense of foreboding settling over us like the dust at sunset.

Dad drove us home at top speed, the truck jolting and rattling, all of us clinging on for dear life. When he finally pulled up with a screech, next to the house, he told us all to get indoors and lock up and wait for him.

"Where are you going, Ian?" Mom's eyes were wide and her hands shook.

"Don't worry, babe," said Dad, trying to sound reassuring, "I'm just going to take a drive around, check that everything is secure. With Frank in hospital, I've got to make sure everyone knows who is in charge. Now, get inside, all of you!"

The four of us ran into the house like a herd of frightened buck, ears pricked to catch any sound or movement, stepping lightly, our newly frightened eyes surveying the now-dark garden and the bush beyond, before shutting the door with a crash of keys and bolts, flipping every light switch and wrenching the curtains closed.

The dark is rising, I thought to myself. *It's coming.*

The four of us huddled on the red sofa in the living room, waiting.

"Mommy," whimpered Jessie, "I'm scared. What's happening? Where's Dad? Are they going to cut him and kill him like that man on TV?"

"They'll never be able to do that to *my* dad!" shouted Luke fiercely. "He's too big and strong for them – he could shoot them all dead, he could! And he will, he will, if any of them try it!" And he buried his little face in Mom's chest and bawled.

After what felt like a lifetime, we heard a banging at the door and Dad's voice shouting, "Open up! Open the door!" Mom burst into tears again and I jumped up to let Dad in. He filled the hallway with his scent of tobacco, sweat and wood smoke, his face red. I ran to get some water and a face towel and he flopped down in the nearest chair.

"There's more of them, bloody squatters, down by the orchard. Looks like they just arrived. Roasting mielies and drinking beer, the bloody cheek!"

Mom handed Dad a stiff drink.

"It'll take some work, getting rid of this new bunch," said Dad at last. "They looked like a bunch of vagrants, to be honest, far too young to be war vets, half of them drunk already …"

Then we heard the sound of drums and singing, floating out towards us from the orchard.

Mom shivered and pressed her hand to her lips. "Oh, Ian," she sobbed, "what are we going to do?"

Dad held her as she buried her face in his shoulder. The twins began to cry too and we all held on to each other, tears rolling down our faces, hearts thumping in our chests, listening to the liberation songs, strong on the night air.

The papers said that, at the Independence Day celebrations, the President had called land 'the last colonial question', and said that he was determined to resolve it 'once and for all'.

It looked to me like the blacks were going about doing just that.

27
Damage control

How to describe the days that followed?

We were constantly on the phone to our family, to other farming families, advising them on how best to secure their property, how to make sure staff were loyal, what to do in case of an invasion, legal action they could take.

"It's like the war all over again, Ian," said Mom, and I knew she was talking about that suffocating feeling of being under siege, of being surrounded by an enemy that, at any moment, could descend on you and rip your life to shreds. Only this time there was no Rhodesian Army to defend us.

The President was behind the Land Redistribution Programme, the laws had already been changed to make way for land reform and Dad said that the police were all corrupt, that the judges were being shuffled like a pack of cards, and that the local people were complicit with the 'war vets'. It made sense to me: after all, they were black and we were white.

We didn't stand a chance.

We began to crumble, slowly at first. Uncle Paul lost his plea and was forced to pack up the old house – all our memories, one hundred years of our family's history – in twenty days, surrounded by 'war vets' shouting threats, shooting at the dogs, harassing the farm workers.

But Uncle Paul was staunch. He held his head up as he went about dismantling the farm infrastructure, arranging for the transport of the animals. "I'll be damned if they get hold of everything we worked so hard for," he declared, his eyes dark. "They want the land? They can have the land – but only the land, nothing more!"

The government had offered to compensate Uncle Paul for improvements made to the land - but he couldn't take the tobacco harvest with him. In the confusion, the tobacco plants were neglected and, soon enough, the crop began to wither and waste away. Harvest time came and went and the fields lay heaving, sighing under a sea of dying tobacco leaves.

Grandad cried when he saw that. "In all my years as a farmer," he sniffed, "I have never seen such waste, such heartbreaking waste. If this is a sign of things to come, I pity the people of this country. They will bring the whole country to its knees, you see if they don't."

Later, when Grandad died of a heart attack, one month after they all arrived in South Africa, they said he died of a broken heart. Losing the farm and everything he had worked so hard for had been the last straw.

Gran just wept continuously, her eyes raw, as she wiped the dust off the family photographs that had lined the mantelpiece, before wrapping them in newspapers that spoke of the Land Redistribution Programme – the Third Chimurenga – as a means of sharing the fruits of independence with the majority, of righting historical wrongs. But Dad said that the farms were being seized by government officials to enrich themselves and their allies, and that the ordinary people wouldn't get a look in.

But while Uncle Paul, Auntie Bernadette and the rest of the family prepared to leave their farm, Dad fought to keep ours.

He tried everything: speaking for the first time to our local MP – a man whose existence we had not even been aware of prior to this - filling in forms, giving up parts of the farm, offering to divide it up. But Dad's reputation as a 'hard *baas*' preceded him – and no one was willing to step in and help us out.

For the first time since just after independence, Mom and Dad, and everyone we knew, began to follow the radio news, the television news, and began reading the national paper. Among all the pro-Party, self-congratulatory, chest-thumping articles, there was news, real news that related directly to us.

Farms were being invaded all over the country; the government had decided that it would no longer take action against squatters; the opposition party, the Movement for Democratic Change, was condemned and accused of puppetry due to its close involvement with the Commercial Farmers' Union; the BBC was banned from reporting from inside Zimbabwe, and its reports disappeared from the main news at eight.

I saw that Rudo's father, the government minister, was also championing the farm invasions. "This is a historic opportunity to right the wrongs of the past," he was quoted as saying.

Well, Rudo, I thought bitterly. *I hope you are happy now.*

One night, after a particularly frustrating day, Dad sat in his chair, morose, drinking glass after glass of Scotch.

"Ian," Mom whispered in a voice watery with tears, "what are we going to do?"

Dad said nothing, frowning as he smoked his cigarette.

"Did you hear me?" Mom's voice had a hysterical edge to it and I glanced at Luke who continued to snore, his thumb in his mouth. "What the hell are we going to do?"

"I don't know!" exploded Dad, getting up to pace the room. "I don't bloody know, all right? I'm doing everything I can to get us out of this – but it's like swimming against the tide! Every time we launch a defence, they shoot it down with laws and bylaws. The guys over at the Commercial Farmers' Union are working with those MDC guys but they've not been able to make any difference! If I could answer that question, we wouldn't be in this bloody mess!"

And he stormed out to the veranda where he stood staring out into the night sky, looking for answers.

Dad began to drink heavily each night, falling into a stupor on the sofa where Patience would find him the next morning, irritable due to a hangover and a terrible crick in his neck from having slept against the sofa arm. He took his frustration out on the workers, many of whom seemed about to leave at any moment. They were scared, I think, scared of ending up like Frank.

One morning, Dad woke up in a particularly foul mood. He shouted at Patience as she tried to clean the living room and ordered her to get out. He barked at Jessie when she tried to kiss him good morning and he smacked Luke for wetting the bed again.

"Ian," Mom said reproachfully. "You are not helping by lashing out at the kids. They can't cope any more – I can't cope any more..."

"Oh, spare me the drama, Sue!" Dad shouted. "I'm not in the mood!"

Mom looked stunned, as if he had just slapped her across the face. "I mean it, Ian," she said after a pause, her lip quivering. "I want to leave. I want us to leave, to take the kids to Harare, just until things blow over..."

"Never!" Dad roared, his hands balled into fists. "Never let me hear you say that again! Do you think I'm going to roll over and accept defeat? Let these bloody people have their victory? Never! I'd rather die..."

"Well, maybe you'd rather I died, Ian!" Mom's face was pinched with bitterness. "Maybe you'd rather we all died! You are putting our lives at risk, all because of your stupid pride!" She ran from the room, sobbing.

Dad cursed and walked over to the drinks cabinet, his shoulders heaving.

"Dad," I whispered foolishly, "isn't it a bit early..?"

"That's enough, Katie," he spat, turning away from me. "Haven't you got anything better to do than stand there lecturing me? Go look after your brother and sister, see if your mom is OK..."

Tears stinging my eyes, I slipped out of the room.

Later that day, the garden boy felt the sting of Dad's *sjambok.* He had done something minor, used the wrong chemical in the pool or something, and Dad really let him have it. He lost control, the pressure of the difficult weeks finally finding an outlet. I couldn't bear to look at the boy when Dad finally threw the whip down and stomped off, muttering about a stiff Scotch. Patience and Grace had to carry the boy back to the workers' quarters.

So you see, our family was disintegrating even before they finally took over our farm.

For weeks now, the farm had been inhabited by pockets of people, squatting in makeshift houses, grazing their cows and goats on our land, ploughing up the earth to plant maize and *rapoko*. And every time the 'war vets' came singing, there were more of them. Soon, they were bold enough to come to the orchard and take what they wanted. They had been told by the 'war vets' that our farm was on the list to be redistributed. As far as they were concerned, it was a done deal.

The next day, Dad made one last desperate effort.

Dressed in his best suit, he gathered up title deeds, lawyers' letters, accounts, pay slips and maps of the surrounding land, jumped in the car and drove all the way to Harare, to the law courts there, to appeal against the government's decision to seize our farm.

But he picked the wrong day to go.

If only we had known, things might not have turned out the way they did.

But then again, maybe it wouldn't have changed anything.

Maybe it was inevitable.

It happened at around nine o'clock that evening. The twins were in bed and Mom and I were sitting in front of the television, waiting for Dad to get back from town. His voice on the phone had been colourless, sapped of strength, and we did not expect good news. Mom had been drinking brandy and her face was flushed, her speech slurred.

The 'war vets' had not come for a few days and we expected a night of peace. Until we heard the familiar sound of their songs floating across the garden. The dogs started growling, baring their teeth. As the sound grew closer, they began barking and got up to patrol the front door.

Dad! I screamed in my head. *Where are you?*

Then there was a loud knocking at the door.

Mom swore and slammed her drink down on the table. "I've had enough of this!" she screamed as she barged past me to the front door.

"Mom!" I cried, panic rising in my chest. "What are you doing? Come back here!" I ran after her, my bare feet slapping on the cold floor.

But she was already at the front door, wrenching it open, panting with the effort of sliding back the enormous bolt.

Then the door was open, and the porch light lit up a group of about ten men and women, squatters, led by Comrade Zvinobaya. Beside him, his face still painfully swollen, his body tense and angry, was the garden boy.

"What the bloody hell do you want?" bellowed Mom, in a raw, hoarse voice, a voice so unlike her own it made me want to cover my ears and run to my room. But I stayed put.

Comrade Zvinobaya answered her coolly. "Where is the old man?"

"None of your bloody business," hissed Mom through gritted teeth.

Comrade Zvinobaya's brow furrowed above his glasses. "This is very serious," he said gravely. "We are here to talk to him about his treatment of one of his workers." He nodded towards the garden boy, who looked right at Mom, his eyes flashing.

Mom faltered when she saw the gardener looking at her like that, one of his eyes swollen shut, his lip cut.

"I've always tried to do good work for you, Madam," his eyes seemed to be saying. "And this is how you repay me."

But Mom's mind was foggy with the drink and she couldn't decide how to respond. So she drew herself up. "*Baas* is coming back from town now-now, with court order. So you'd better *faga moto,* hurry up, and get off this *stoep* before *baas* gets back or you'll be sorry!" Her courage was buoyed by the alcohol that flowed through her system, and she didn't notice how her tone, her words, incensed Comrade Zvinobaya.

He frowned and spat to the side. "We won't allow him to continue to abuse his workers!" he shouted. "They have rights and there are laws to protect them. Tell your husband that he cannot behave as if he is above the law any more, that this type of treatment will not be tolerated in an independent Zimbabwe."

Mom started laughing then, a high, drunken laugh as if she had never heard anything so funny. "You wait till he hears you say that," she giggled. "He'll give you more of the same! As far as he is concerned, this is still Rhodesia!"

Then an older woman stepped forward. I hadn't noticed her before because she was dressed in orange overalls like the others and she wore a knitted hat on her head. The men stood back, clearly respecting her position, whatever it was.

Very calmly, she looked Mom in the eye and said, "You are drunk. You don't know what you are saying. Go inside to your children. And start packing your things. Your notice to quit is almost up. This land is being given back to its rightful owners and that's final. Screaming abuse won't change that – but it could make some of our comrades very angry..." She swept her hand to the side to indicate the others. "Do you see these men here? Most of them fought in the Chimurenga. Some of them lost their families, some lost use of their limbs, all of them missed years of school. They are hungry. They are angry. And they will not wait any more. So I am telling you, as a mother, stop putting yourself and your family in danger. Go inside now and start packing..."

"What?" shrieked Mom, incensed at the woman's calm and confident tone. "How dare you speak to me like that? Who do you think you are, hey? Someone needs to teach you some manners, some respect!"

The woman looked at Mom for a long moment, her mouth open to show the gap between her front teeth, then shrugged her shoulders and turned away.

Comrade Zvinobaya pushed his way forward. "Now it is time for justice, *true* justice to be done for the people of this country!"

The others all cheered and began to sing again.

Mom curled her lip, swaying slightly. "You bloody idiot, d'you have any idea what you're saying? Or are you just repeating the lies that your corrupt leaders have been telling you?!" She leaned forward and shouted: "You're a bloody *munt*! A dirty, lazy, no-good *munt*, that's what you are!"

I felt faint. I couldn't believe this was happening, couldn't believe Mom was standing at our front door, taunting this ex-soldier, swearing, calling him every name she and our friends joked about, every insult, every jibe, as if she wanted him to go ahead and blow her head off.

The rest of them had stopped singing and were staring at Mom, this crazy white woman who was likening them to baboons, dogs, monkeys and worse. So this was it, in the raw, how we really saw them. I think they were shocked to hear it for themselves, yelled out by a drunk white 'madam', right there on land they had claimed as their own.

Comrade Zvinobaya struggled to regain control of the situation. When Mom kept screaming, he grabbed her by her arm.

Mom stopped shouting abruptly and looked down, horrified, at the dark brown fingers biting into the white flesh of her upper arm. "You get your filthy hands off me…" she breathed. Then she spat, full and wet, in Comrade Zvinobaya's face. "Stinking *kaffir*!"

That was when he slapped her. She reeled momentarily, then swung her arm and slapped him back. With a grim look on his face, he grabbed her shoulders and pushed her, hard, against the cabinet that stood just inside the front door.

Mom stumbled and crashed into the heavy wood. I ran to her side then, sobbing.

"Ah, *vakomana*." Comrade Zvinobaya turned away. "This is one of the really bad ones..."

I was so busy seeing to Mom, helping her up, that I didn't notice when they melted into the night.

"Get me another drink, Katie," slurred Mom, her fingers shaking as she struggled to light a cigarette.

I stared at her. She was really out of it. I still couldn't believe what had just happened, let alone think about what might have happened if the 'comrades' had been drunk or high. Or armed.

"I'm going to bed," I said shortly. I didn't trust myself to say more.

Mom waved me away, the brandy sloshing over the sides of her glass, the cigarette butt glowing orange as she sucked at it.

I looked in on the twins on my way to my room. Luke turned and whimpered in his sleep. I thought of my bedroom and how it still smelled of Sheba. I knew I didn't want to sleep on my own that night. I climbed into bed next to Luke and rested my cheek on his hair, my arms encircling him from behind. I was soon fast asleep.

I was woken by someone shaking me. My mind reeled as I tried to make sense of what was happening. I could smell urine and feel dampness on my jeans – Luke had had another accident. But I could also smell smoke, bitter and pungent in my nostrils. And the dark shape shaking me was Patience, the maid.

"Come," she said urgently. "The house is burning."

I can't describe the fear, the horror, of seeing flames, raw flames, eating away at the building around you – your home – while you rush to and fro, trying to wake sleepy children, thinking of running back to save your book collection, or your dolls or your photo albums, yet knowing that you can't, that you must leave everything behind.

Already the flames had climbed to the roof and the noise of roaring flames and breaking beams was deafening. The bedrooms were starting to fill with smoke and we coughed and spluttered as Patience and I wrapped Luke and Jessie in quilts and picked them up, trying to hush their hysterical crying. In the passageway, fire licked along the floor, devouring the old rugs. The glass on Grandma's watercolour paintings shattered, shards of glass landing on us and the children. I felt them slice my feet as I ran over them towards the entrance but I didn't stop.

"Where's Mom?" I shouted, my voice muffled by the shirt I held over my mouth.

"She's safe, madam," shouted Patience. "I got her out already."

Just then, the main beam supporting the banister crashed to the floor beside us in a shower of sparks. Towards the front of the house, the heat was unbearable and I struggled to breathe, my sweat-slicked hands clutching at Jessie. But the way out was barred by a roaring wall of fire.

We turned back, stumbling, until we reached the guest bedroom at the end of the house. Once inside, Patience collapsed against the door, wheezing. "I can't do it, madam. I breathe too much smoke… you go… take the children…"

"No, Patience!" I yelled, shaking her. "We can make it… hold on!"

Patience nodded silently, her eyes closed. She held on to the twins who huddled around her, sniffling.

I grabbed towels from the cupboard and piled them against the bottom of the door to keep the smoke out. Then I rifled through the drawers to find the key to the garden door.

"Katie?" quavered Jessie. "I'm scared! Where's Mom? Where's Dad? What's happening?"

My fingers closed on the keys and I uttered a silent prayer. In moments, I had the back door open and was carrying Luke and Jessie out to the pool where Mom lay sprawled on a blanket, her mouth slack, her hair stuck to her forehead.

Then I went back to drag Patience out.

The house glowed against the night sky with a terrible beauty. The flames and showers of sparks reflected in the tears in my eyes as I stared at what was left of my childhood home.

At least we were all safe, I told myself. That was what mattered.

Dad found us huddled by the pool in the early hours of the morning.

"What the...?" He stood in front of the smoking remains of the house, his shoulders shaking, his hands balled into fists.

"The bastards!" he screamed, his face contorted with anguish, sinking to his knees.

Then I realised. He thought the squatters had done it. And none of us said anything. Mom looked at me guiltily with her bloodshot eyes, Patience glanced away. But none of us said a thing.

So there was nothing to do but pack ourselves into the *bakkie* and drive, drive, drive away from there.

The court had refused Dad's appeal. The farm was to be redistributed and there was nothing we could do about it. They got everything: the horses, the cattle, all the produce in the fields, and the land, of course. The precious land that they kept going on about. It was theirs at last.

Mom cried as she told everyone about her encounter with the war vets that night, about how terrified she had been, how she had stood up to them, how they had assaulted her and set fire to the house. Everyone was horrified and sympathetic – 'But what do you expect? These guys are savages, man…'

And I never said anything. I didn't talk about how drunk Mom was, about how she had provoked the squatters, sworn at them, spat at them, dared them to do their worst. And I could not get rid of a small, hard knot inside me, somewhere near my heart. A hard knot of anger and bitterness that made me grind my teeth and refuse to speak.

Because I couldn't get that image out of my head: Mom, drunk as a lord on brandy, struggling with a box of matches and a cigarette

PART 3

Tariro and Katie

Zimbabwe 2001

28
Ex-combatant

It is a moonlit night and my heart is uneasy. Comrade Justice says that we cannot wait any longer, that we must go into the village tonight. But my heart tells me that this is the wrong decision.

We are crawling through the bush on our bellies, the dry grass and earth shifting and scratching against our khaki trousers, mirroring the song of the crickets. We keep our heads down as we follow each other, men and women, comrades in arms, through the darkness of the bush, towards food and shelter.

At the thought of food, I feel faint and my stomach rumbles, loud enough to disturb the birds roosting in the trees far above us. We have not eaten in days. My heels are cracked and bleeding, my legs and forearms covered in festering sores that refuse to heal. We ran out of water two days ago and the sweat and dust clings to me like a second skin. It is hard to keep our spirits up under these conditions.

At the sight of the village ahead, my heart trembles. I know this place! Yes, I can see our house, where Tawona was born and… and I can see Baba! And Babamunini! There they are, sitting by the fire, taking their snuff.

Who is this coming towards them? Can it really be? Yes, it is! My heart races as I see Amai, my mother, walking towards my father, one hand supporting her pregnant belly, the other holding a plate. I know what is in that plate: Amai's famous goat meat stew and sadza.

I am so close, I can smell it.

I open my mouth to call to her: Amai, ndadzoka! I have returned!

And then I hear the terrible juddering overhead, slicing through the night air, and the stomach-wrenching whine of death delivered from above.

Right before my eyes, the houses burst into flame; beneath me, the ground shakes and, flung apart by the impact of the bomb, I see the bodies of Baba, Babamunini, Amai, sprawled, mangled, bleeding.

The scent of fresh blood, burning thatch and goat-meat stew hit me full in the face and I begin to vomit…

I woke up with a start, retching, my heart pounding, sweat clinging to my brow. A dream. Just a dream. Based on a nightmare past, but just a dream all the same.

"Tariro?" My husband stirred beside me, his hand reaching for mine in the dark. "Are you OK?"

I swallowed hard and passed my hand over my face. "It's all right, Nhamo," I said, trying to stop my voice from trembling. "I'm fine."

He held me silently, knowing that whatever I had seen would stay locked forever in my memory, silenced. I did not want to cause pain to anyone, to burden anyone with my memories, least of all my beloved Nhamo.

Yes, Nhamo.

We did get married in the end. I smile to think of it, even now. For while I was away in the bush, fighting for our freedom, Nhamo was preparing himself for independence by learning to read with his fingertips, equipping himself to teach others, to help blind children pursue their studies, in spite of their blindness.

When he once again sent a *munyai* to ask for me, in 1979, when our leaders were in talks to secure independence, Baba wept with remorse for what had gone before. Even Mainini Tambudzai shed a few tears. We had lost so much time, Nhamo was handicapped and Amai was no more. It was a bittersweet reunion.

So we finally got married after waiting all those years to be together.

And we had a child, a son, who grew up with Tawona as his sister. Nhamo took care of her like one of his own. I wondered many times whether it was his blindness that allowed him to love her so fearlessly. Perhaps if he had been able to see her golden skin and blue, blue eyes, he would have guessed who her father was. And perhaps his anger towards the man who had robbed him of his sight – and so much more – would have overwhelmed him. But he could not see and he never asked. And I never said. I still felt guilty, you see. It had all happened because of me. But it was something unspoken between us; just like my time in the bush.

I was one of the lucky ones; I was able to return from the war and live a normal life; I was able to love again, to have a family. Not all of us ex-combatants were as fortunate.

There were days when I could pretend that I had never carried an AK-47 in the mountains of Mozambique. That I had never looked into the eyes of a Rhodesian soldier before squeezing the trigger and seeing the terror of what a bullet at close range can do. That I had never seen my brother Farai's unburied body, shot and mutilated and paraded as a 'terrorist' by the Rhodesian Army.

There were days when I could forget.

But even on the days when memories tormented me and invaded my sleep, I told no one. None of us did.

In those heady years after independence, education, real education, was finally made available to all, not just the white minority. I went to agricultural college. We learned the science of farming, knowledge that added to what we knew in our bones: how to nurture the land, the benefits of crop rotation and how to research our market and calculate annual profits.

We were all preparing for the time when we would be farmers again, on our own soil once more, even though the Lancaster House Agreement meant that the government could not take land by force. This was the 1980s and the government had to wait for a willing seller, one who would charge market rates. But the whites held on to the land. Most of them did not grow food to feed the people of Zimbabwe; they were busy growing tobacco and tea for export, running dairy farms, growing hectares of oranges in the valley.

So we, the landless majority, had to wait patiently, even when the World Bank began to squeeze us and we tasted the misery of economic reforms. By then our dreams of having our land returned to us were blurred by hunger and scarcity, by the strange taste of yellow *sadza* and thousands losing their jobs in the public sector. The dream of the land seemed far away then.

Until the Third Chimurenga. What the BBC called the 'land invasions'. Land invasions? How does one invade land that is yours by right? Land for which you have waited for over 20 years? The white farmers were finally told, once and for all, that the land question would have to be resolved, and we ex-combatants dared to believe that we would have what we had fought so hard for.

When the Land Redistribution Programme began, we applied for land near Masvingo. We had a strong case. Our people had been pushed off our ancestral land to make way for white farmers, I had fought in the war and I had training and experience in farming. Along with Nhamo's nephews and my brothers' and sisters' children, we were a large family, more than capable of running a large farm.

Eventually, we were granted land in the area where our people had once lived, near to my childhood home.

Our family had finally returned.

29
No place like home

Like so many other white families, we decided to leave Zimbabwe. Most of Dad's money had been tied up in the farm and, after a while, it became clear that we were not going to be compensated. So money was tight.

We heard that Britain was offering asylum to those fleeing the land invasions, and Mom didn't want to go to South Africa. She wanted to be near her sister, Janie, who had already moved to London with Uncle Mannie. So Dad obliged.

But I never thought the adjustment would be so hard.

When we reached London, we were greeted by rain, English rain, gloomy and promising nothing but grey skies and dark, wet streets.

Flying high over London, the sky was almost the same blue as back home but, as we began our descent through the thick grey clouds, rain began to mist the plane's windows. By the time we were bumping along the runway, the grey had set in, damp and heavy. We shivered as we made our way through the great, grey, terminal building – a halting family with mismatched, too-light coats and startled expressions.

Mom tried her best to maintain her poise but even she was intimidated by the length of the corridors, the sheer size of the place. By the time we got to the immigration desk and told them that we were seeking asylum, that we had lost our farm in Zimbabwe, she looked as frightened and out of place as we did.

At the Arrivals gate, our eyes scanned the crowd, searching desperately for a familiar face.

"Sue!" The voice was unmistakable. It was Auntie Janie. Mom turned towards the voice and tears sprang to her eyes as she rushed forward, her arms outstretched, to be greeted by her sister, pressing her lips together to keep from crying out.

"I'm sorry, hey," Auntie Janie whispered into Mom's travel-weary hair, her smoker's voice as throaty as Mom's. "I'm so sorry." They held each other for a long time.

Uncle Mannie stepped towards us, tall and sombre in an expensive-looking dark wool coat.

He stuck his hand out and Dad grasped it, shaking it firmly, blinking back tears, not wanting to cry in front of Uncle Mannie. The rest of us huddled round him. I could feel Jessie shaking with tears held in too long and I picked her up so that she could bury her face in my shoulder. She wiped her runny nose on my jacket.

"Jeez, guys," Uncle Mannie said at last. "Too bad, hey?" He had never been good with words.

Then Auntie Janie turned to us and knelt down, her arms open wide. We all hugged her as she stroked our hair. "You poor, poor children," she was crooning. "It'll be all right, you'll see…"

Uncle Mannie looked at the pitifully small pile of bags on our trolley. "That all you got?" he asked, incredulous.

Mom drew herself up to her full height. "It was all we could get away with," she said meaningfully.

Uncle Mannie shrugged and started wheeling the trolley towards the exit. "The car's this way," he called.

The council gave us a flat, on the fourth floor of

a council building, in the middle of a huge housing estate. The sight of those high-rises, the stench of the lift, was so different to anything I had ever known that it was almost too much for me. I would have fainted if I had not been holding Jessie. I had to be strong.

So we moved into this dark, poky flat, with mildew staining the walls, and tried to call it home.

"What time will you be home?"

"Come, we'll eat them at home."

"This bloody rain! I can't wait to get home."

But we were just lying to each other. Lying to ourselves.

This was not home.

Mornings at home were busy: Mom having her morning coffee, hair in curlers, shouting after the maid; Dad rustling the paper, checking the tobacco prices; Luke and Jessie wolfing down baked beans, eggs and *boerewors*, our spicy local sausage; Patience pouring out hot tea, packing our lunches; the gardener bringing in the first of the day's crop from Mom's garden, tomatoes, avocados, guavas.

Then the rush to clamber up into the back of the truck on the weekend before term began, fresh in the morning mist, school jerseys and blazers and knee-high socks and Radio Three. The dew-draped acacia trees flashing past, spiders' webs sparkling in the long, dry grass, the sky blue and wide and forever over your head.

That was home.

Here, in our flat in London, mornings were chaotic but in a quiet, stifled sort of way. Dad was depressed. Mom just wasn't used to managing on her own. Her oatmeal porridge was lumpy; our sandwiches were the same every day. And I couldn't drink her tea – it tasted like dishwater.

Dad started drinking heavily again, and the dreary fumes from his cigarettes hung over us like a cloud, blotting out everything that used to shine.

School was a big adjustment too.I never thought I would miss that hot, stiff blazer, the compulsory sports, the deference to prefects and teachers that were the hallmarks of life at St Paul's. But I did. I missed my teachers, I missed the other girls in the boarding hostel, and I missed singing in the choir. I even found myself missing Rudo – her wry humour, the smell of her deodorant, whispering after lights-out – although I chided myself about that: wasn't she enjoying someone's stolen farm, along with her corrupt minister father and rugby-playing brother, Max? It made no sense for me to miss her – but I did.

30
Homecoming

It rained the day we came home.

As we drove along the winding road, the granite-topped hills and baobab trees flashing past, I saw again the landscape of my childhood. While everyone else talked and laughed, singing along to the songs on the radio, I retreated into myself. I was fourteen again, squeezed on to the back of a truck, pressed against Amai's pregnant belly, my eyes still stinging from the smoke and the tears, surrounded by wailing, lamenting women and children, men who cried silent tears or hid their sorrow behind masks of courage.

And it struck me then that I was the only one in the car who had seen these hills when we first made this journey, when we were first exiled to the Tribal Trust Lands. Nhamo had lost his sight by then, and none of the others had been born.

I looked at the young people, at my son, now almost a man, and my heart fluttered. Did they have any idea of what this meant, this return to the land of our ancestors? With their British-style education and taste for American music, I wasn't sure whether we had done enough to pass this dream on to them, whether we had planted the seeds of love and loyalty deep enough in their hearts.

"The youth of today are selfish!" said MaiFungai, my neighbour. "Do you think these 'born-frees' care about the land or the past? All they want is an easy life, to get rich quick or leave the country – the life of a farmer is not for them, even if it is land that their parents fought and died for."

"No, MaiFungai," I had replied, shaking my head. "You must not be so negative. We must have faith in our youth, they are the future of this country."

MaiFungai had laughed harshly and clapped her hands. "Then God help this country, MaiTawona, God help us!"

Then I had said, "If our youth are lazy or lack conviction, it is because we, the parents, didn't teach them properly." But I knew that there was more to it than that. Parents can only do so much – we cannot change the schooling system, or the economy or the government.

I shook my head. These were gloomy thoughts,

depressing thoughts that had no place in my head today. I looked out of the window at the *kopjes* and Hondo, my son, reached over and squeezed my hand.

We drove slowly up the dirt road, the overgrown savannah grass on either side scratching against the sides of the car.

'That will need to be cut back,' I thought to myself, aware of a swelling in my chest at the thought of this responsibility, this great work before us.

We drove past the fading sign – 'Baobab Ranch' – and through the rusted metal gates, past the site of the old farmhouse towards the outbuildings. We had already been told that we would have to build our house from scratch as the farmhouse had been destroyed by fire.

"Knowing these whites, they did it on purpose because they couldn't stand the thought of blacks living there," the officer sniffed when he told us. We had nodded, unsurprised. But a new house cost money to build so we would have to make do with the outbuildings, until we were able to save up. We parked the car and everyone got out, stretching their limbs.

The rain had stopped. All I could hear was the sound of raindrops dripping, falling to the ground, the trees sighing with them. The swimming pool was nearly empty, just some greenish black water lying stagnant at the bottom. The flower garden was overgrown with weeds and the lawn grass was brown and patchy. I shook my head. How much water had been used to keep that lawn green, to keep that pool full? I was suddenly aware of the enormity of what had taken place, of the possibilities and the challenges, the huge work that lay ahead.

I found Nhamo's arm. He held my hand tenderly and whispered, "It smells different here. Is it like when we were young? Is it like I remember?"

I bit my lip to stop the tears that threatened to fall. "No, Nhamo," I whispered back. "It is different. Totally different."

He nodded silently and I patted his hand, my heart aching for him, for what he had missed all these years.

Hondo frowned as he looked over at the outbuildings: the maids' quarters, the workers' compound, the stables where they must have kept horses, everything abandoned and shabby-looking. "I will build you a new house one day, Amai," he said. "It will be the most beautiful house you have ever seen."

I smiled at him. "I don't need a beautiful house, *mwanangu*," I said. "As long as I have my family around me, I can live in a tin shack. It won't make any difference. Now I want to walk, to see our land."

"But Amai, it's been raining!" Rufaro, one of Nhamo's nieces cried.

I chuckled. These city kids!

Nhamo laughed too and we both took off our shoes, put on our bush hats and began to walk, holding hands, like we always did.

We walked barefoot to the rain-soaked fields – miraculously ours once again – my wrapper around my waist, my bush hat on my head, the air ripe with the scent of hot, wet earth. Nhamo, my beloved, our children and relatives walked with us. As we walked, the skies began to clear and, soon, the sun was shining onto the steaming earth.

A deep happiness settled into my bones as I picked up the clods of earth and felt their warmth through my fingers, just as I used to do, so long ago. And Nhamo and I, we laughed, me showing the gap between my teeth that had made me the envy of the village, he shaking the stick that was his eyes. We laughed our joy at the fulfillment of our life's dream, of our answered prayers, that we had lived to taste the freedom of walking on our own soil, in the land of our ancestors once again.

Of course we knew there would be troubles ahead: the land reclamation and the redistribution programme that had followed were controversial; there was talk of sanctions, of regime change and, in the city, there was violence and political unrest. But here, out here, we were oblivious to how the world viewed us. As far as we were concerned, this was the justice we had waited for.

"We will make this farm a success, my children," I said, looking around me at the fields covered in dead and dying maize plants, at the cattle pens beyond. "It will be difficult and there will be times when we feel like giving up – but this is the land of your ancestors; we must honour their memory. We must work hard and be productive…"

"And plant pumpkins," added Nhamo, chuckling.

At the mention of pumpkins, tears stung my eyes, my heart flooding with thoughts of Amai. She would have been so happy to witness this day. All of a sudden, I felt the urge to walk westwards, past the line of trees that had been planted as a windbreak, a line of trees I did not recognise.

As I neared the trees I began to run, my joints crying out, but unable to stop. It was as if a force was pulling me, calling to me.

And when I got to the clump of trees, I finally knew why.

For there before me, as tall and wide as it had always been, was Amai's baobab tree, my birthplace. That was when I broke down and cried, weeping tears of sorrow, for Amai, for Baba, for Farai, buried in unkind, foreign places, lonely, so far from the graves of our ancestors; for Nhamo, for Tawona, for all of us who had lost so much, who had endured so much.

But these were tears tinged with joy. For I also felt an elation, a sense of completion, a settling in my soul.

"Yes, Amai," I whispered through my tears. "I have come home. Your daughter has finally come home."

31
Asylum Seekers

Like scrounging beggars, we were granted asylum; we got housing benefit, free places in the local state schools, signed on for Income Support, learned how to use the bus system.

What a change from our former life. Can you imagine?

Mom and Dad hardly spoke any more. When they did, it was in tense, clipped tones.

"Did you buy milk?"

"Have you heard from Paul?"

"The lights aren't working! Did you pay the bill?"

"Ag, this food tastes like kak, man, Sue! Can't you do any better?"

"Well, if you don't like it, you know what you can do about it, Ian!" Veiled threats.

At first we saw Auntie Janie and Uncle Mannie quite a lot, but after a while Dad couldn't stand it any more. Uncle Mannie was so patronising, even offering to get Dad a job in an office, suggesting he go back to school.

"A man's got to have some pride," growled Dad when he got home after our last visit to their house.

"Especially if that's all he's got," retorted Mom curtly, throwing her handbag down on the worn settee.

She started doing that a lot, making cruel, caustic comments aimed at Dad, as if he had let us down. It was as if she was soothing her guilt by making him feel bad. Besides, our family tragedy was now world news; we were part of a historical event, joined through circumstance to other families suffering too, struggling with the realisation that we hadn't just lost our homes; we had lost our identities too.

One day at school we had swimming. But Mom had forgotten to pack my towel so, after the session, I just stood there, shivering, hoping the coach would notice.

Instead, a black girl named Chevonne looked over at me, then held out her towel.

I hesitated. Share a towel with a black girl?

But she saw my reluctance and her eyes narrowed. "Just who d'you think you are?" She kissed her teeth, looking at me, disgusted.

One of the other black girls sneered, "This ain't South Africa, y'know, where you can treat black people like dirt…"

I opened my mouth to say, 'I'm from Zimbabwe, not South Africa,' but they weren't listening. "Make sure you slap her face next time, yeah?"

"Racist cow!"

I ran away from their jeers, trying to hide my tears, thinking of Rudo. All I could see was the look on her face when I walked away from her on the last day of school. I had been ashamed of her. How the tables had turned.

Chevonne was right: who did I think I was?

Not private-schooled, privileged and pampered by servants any more. Not more civilised, more intelligent, more beautiful than anyone else, black or white. Just a girl from a family of poor political refugees, asylum seekers from a land-locked African country, no different to those other people who crowded the Home Office. The only difference was we were white and they weren't.

Our sun-toughened skin and foreign accents marked us as different from white English people – if we had hoped to blend in, to assimilate, we had been sorely mistaken. We were outsiders, people with no home to call their own, holding out our hands for whatever we could get: money, support, acceptance.

We fumbled, looking for answers.

Mom looked for answers in her own way. She took to disappearing during the day. With her bus pass, she rode on the flame-red double-decker buses to Central London where she spent the days wandering Harrods, Selfridges and Harvey Nichols, looking at all the things she would buy once we had our own place again, once we got back on our feet.

She spent hours trying on designer clothes, as if she was a South African diamond heiress, not the wife of a ruined Zimbabwean farmer who drank cheap beer to forget, forget, forget. And she started going to see Auntie Janie on her own, without us, sometimes for daytime visits, other times to go out for drinks and to the theatre, just like they used to back home.

One day, I came home early from school to find her sitting on the sofa in the lounge, on the phone, laughing in a way I hadn't heard for months. She stopped as soon as she saw me and said a hasty goodbye.

"Who was that on the phone, Mom?" I asked, trying to sound nonchalant while a dark feeling crept over my heart.

"Oh, just an old friend I met at your auntie's house," she replied, her voice light, too light, her eyes looking everywhere but at me. She left the room quickly, as if she had just remembered that she had to go and get something. But I will never forget the expression on her face. An expression of renewed hope, of light at the end of the tunnel. And, after that phone call, Mom started using her anti-wrinkle cream again, lathering her hands with the glossy cream that smelled of gardenias and lavender.

If only I had known what that phone call had been about, what it was leading to. I might have been able to stop it.

I don't know why I was the one to meet Mom in the corridor the night she left.

I had woken up to get a glass of water. The flat was still, the noises from outside dulled by the double glazing. As I stepped out of my room on to the carpet in the hallway, I looked up to see Mom there, standing stock still, staring at me. My eyes must have betrayed my surprise, confusion then, ultimately, comprehension as I took in her heavily made-up face, her short dress, the winter coat with the collar turned up, and her hands that clutched desperately at two small suitcases.

"Mom?" I faltered. "What are you doing? Where are you going?"

She bit her lip as her mobile phone vibrated in her hand. "I'm sorry, Katie, I just can't take it any more. Things have been bad for so long now... I've got to go..."

"No, Mom," I hissed. "You can't do this! It's not fair! We're all in this together, remember?"

"Oh, Katie, don't! I feel bad enough as it is! If there was a way I could take you with me I would – but it's impossible right now. Surely you're old enough to understand that. You'll look after the twins for me, won't you? You're so good with them..." She reached out to me but I stepped away from her. My eyes never left her face, angry, accusing.

"After all Dad did for you, this is the thanks he gets?" I couldn't stop the bitterness that I had always felt towards her welling up inside me. All I cared about at that moment was what this would do to Dad. "He sacrificed everything for you, Mom, gave you everything you wanted. How can you do this to him?"

She looked at me then, a new coldness in her eyes. "You always were jealous of me, weren't you, Katie? Jealous that your father loved me and would do anything for me. Jealous that you would never be able to fill my shoes. Your precious daddy – you always took his side in everything."

The truth of her words stung and I faltered.

She noticed and drew herself up and held her bags tighter. "If you think he's the only one who's sacrificed in this marriage, you've got a lot to learn about being a woman, Katie. I was never meant to rot away on a farm in the countryside. I had dreams of better things, of a bigger life."

And while she said that, I thought, 'Better than us, your own children? Bigger than your family?' I didn't understand, didn't want to understand. It hurt too much to know that she resented us, that she felt that we had held her back from happiness. I let her carry on talking, while I cried inside.

"It was my foolish mistake to marry your father and think that I could change him, make him over to be the man I wanted. I know that now. Your father was prepared to sacrifice me – us! – to hold on to his dream, his precious farm, and look where that got us. I'm sorry, Katie, but now it's my turn to live my dream. It's my turn to be happy."

Then she saw the tears standing in my eyes, my lips pressed together and her shoulders sagged, just a little. "I'm sorry, Katie," she whispered, stepping towards me. "I'm sorry it has to be this way. Maybe, one day, you'll find it in your heart to forgive me." She hugged me then, and I stood like a statue, unyielding. She felt my stiffness and drew away, biting her lip.

I could have made her stay then. I could have begged her and she would have stayed. But I didn't. Part of me was too proud to beg her to have pity on us, to sacrifice her happiness for us. So I said nothing.

"I'll come for you as soon as I can," she whispered, her fingers brushing my cheek. Then she turned and walked out of the front door, dropping the keys through the letterbox, leaving me choking on the bitter taste of my mother's selfishness.

And I was left to pick up the pieces and keep the family together.

After Mom left, Dad began to fade. If losing the farm, his life's work, had begun to destroy him, Mom's leaving finished the job. He started to drink during the day, sometimes at home, other times in the pub down the road. And always, he would get into a fight, swearing about '*bloody kaffirs*' and 'teaching them a lesson they would never forget'. Then he would start crashing into things and crying, and I would tremble inside. He often forgot to go and sign for our money. Then I had to hunt for coins to buy a tin of baked beans for the kids' supper.

One night, he didn't come home. I got a call from the station: he had been in a fight and was being charged with grievous bodily harm. We couldn't pay the bail. He would not be coming home. And we had no more milk in the house, no bread for the next day's sandwiches.

That was when it dawned on me how alone I was.

That was when I cracked.

I reached into my old suitcase, the one I had brought from Zimbabwe. I fished around in the side pocket and brought out a small slip of paper, a paper that Gran had pressed into my palm last year, when she heard that we were planning a visit to England.

As if in a dream, I walked to the phone in the hallway and dialled the number on the slip of paper.

It rang.

On the fifth ring, someone picked up the phone.

He still sounded the same, after all these years.

"Hello?" he said, his voice puzzled. "Who's this?"

"Uncle James?" I whispered, my voice hoarse, teetering on the brink of tears. "It's Katie, Ian's daughter, your niece. Please… help me…"

They came to get us that night, my disgraced Uncle James and his wife, Rutendo, her skin the colour of polished wood, her long dreadlocks tied up in an African print scarf. Ignoring my awkwardness, they packed up our few belongings and carried a disorientated Luke and Jessie to their car.

"Who are they, Katie?" asked Jessie. "Where are they taking us? Are they taking us to Mom?"

"Where's Dad?" demanded Luke. "And who's that black lady?" I buried my head in his hair and shushed him. I didn't have any answers.

I had reached rock bottom.

32
Unfamiliar territory

We arrived at Uncle James's home, fearful, clutching our bags to our chests. My eyes widened when I took in the African masks and bright woven baskets on the walls, the photos of brown-skinned people I didn't know on the mantelpiece – and I looked again at Uncle James's wife, Rutendo.

She stood next to Uncle James, tall and elegant in her black sweater dress, a soft look of compassion on her face. I felt myself strangely drawn to her and, for a moment, I couldn't understand why. Then I realised what it was: she reminded me of Rudo. That same uncomplicated ease, like it was the most natural thing in the world for me to be staying with her, sleeping under her roof, sharing her food.

Rutendo, or Auntie Rutendo, as she introduced herself to us, had won a scholarship to study for a PhD in London. The whole family had come to be with her while she studied. An educated, black Zimbabwean woman, married to my uncle. Imagine that.

"Believe me," Rutendo said later, "we would never have taken the children away from their family and friends – their home – if it wasn't something important."

"Important and temporary," added Uncle James meaningfully. "Zim is where we belong, where we want to raise the kids. We've got a lot of work to do there, especially now that things are so difficult, what with the sanctions, the drought, inflation..."

"We know so many people who've left Zim, saying that the country's been destroyed…"

"But we believe in what they're trying to do; give the wealth back to the people."

"We'll be going back as soon as I finish this PhD," Rutendo stated firmly.

'Going back to what?' I thought to myself. 'I though they wanted to get rid of the whites once and for all…'

Then I remembered that Uncle James wasn't like me and Dad and the rest of our family. Uncle James had nothing to worry about. He had sided with the blacks long ago so I guess he could still see a future in a country with crazy inflation, food shortages and a power-hungry leadership. I felt a sense of satisfaction every time the BBC reported that Mugabe had driven his country to the brink of catastrophe and that the economy had gone into meltdown since the expulsion of the white farmers.

Although I was grateful to Uncle James for rescuing us, for calling the police station and dealing with Dad's arrest, I couldn't help remembering what Dad had called him: a traitor to the race, a disgrace.

To their credit, Luke and Jessie didn't bat an eyelid when they saw Uncle James's children with their brown skin and curly hair. As far as they were concerned, they were just some friendly Zim kids with a roomful of toys and familiar accents. I didn't tell them that they were cousins straight away.

It didn't take long for their laughter to become freer and, soon, I began to recognise a touch of the joyfulness I had often heard when they played back home on the farm, with the horses or with the dogs. They were even rediscovering their old accents and turns of phrase that had been buried by their British comprehensive school. I was glad for them.

Rutendo, Uncle James's wife, was totally cool. She seemed to know that I was having trouble adjusting but I could never have told her that I was having a hard time getting used to the idea of my uncle and her, living in their house, eating *sadza* for dinner, hearing my own uncle speak Shona, realising that their Zimbabwe was a totally different world from mine.

By now, I was used to every person who found out that I was Zimbabwean and used to live on a farm, asking me about how Mugabe kicked us off our land. When I spoke of it, I felt again the hurt and anger and the sense of gross injustice. And I felt validated: I had a story to tell, an important story, a story that was being broadcast all over the news. We were the victims who had been through a terrible ordeal; the blacks were the oppressors, the thieves who stole our homes from us and were now ravaging the land and ruining the country's economy.

But I never spoke about the fire that destroyed our home, or how it started.

Besides, in this house, the dynamic was different. In many subtle ways, I got the impression that Uncle James and his wife did not entirely agree with my version of events – but they were too polite and considerate to challenge me.

But I knew that some members of Rutendo's

family and other people she knew had fought in the bush war and had been granted land under the redistribution programme.

And so, in spite of their generosity, I still felt ill at ease under their roof. There was a huge gulf separating us.

33
Full circle

The new farm was a lot of work, hard but satisfying. The chickens were now laying regularly and we were able to send a batch of eggs into town every other day, for sale in the market there. I had also been rearing chickens and ducks for meat and they were doing well, although the chicken feed had become quite pricey.

"I don't know whether we will see a profit on those chickens, Tariro," Nhamo told me.

"Maybe not," I shrugged, "but it's worth a try."

We had already cleared the land we were going to use to grow food for the family; now we were concentrating on the larger areas, the fields where we would be growing commercial crops for sale in town.

We were all excited, but nervous too. We knew only too well from watching the news that the outside world was waiting for us to fail and fail miserably. 'Everyone knows that Africans can't farm' reverberated in my head each day as we divided up seed, bought fertiliser, established a compost heap and worked out how to acquire a tractor on hire purchase.

We may have had less experience than those who had farmed these large tracts of land before us but what we lacked in know-how, we made up for in sheer hard work, passion and dedication. And we reread our dusty agricultural college textbooks, we asked the more experienced farm workers for advice, we experimented, tried and tested until we came up with solutions to the problems we encountered on a daily basis.

We had appointed Nhamo's eldest nephew, Kuziwa, to be the farm manager as he had also been to agricultural college. He took care of the labour force, hiring workers and managing their daily activities. We were like one enormous family, each one of us feeling responsible for the success of our farm. Those were good days.

And, all around the country, other black families were taking on these new responsibilities as they were granted land to farm. Of course, there were a lot of farms that were grabbed by corrupt individuals and some even lay idle, with no one to manage them.

But that didn't change the fact that the ordinary people of Zimbabwe were at last getting the chance to cultivate the land that was theirs. It was a historic achievement.

One day, I was sitting in the kitchen of the small house we had built, trying to work out a way to grow my chicken business without incurring more debt, when Kuziwa came to the open kitchen door.

"*Go-go-goyi*!" he called from the door, seeking permission to enter.

I looked up and smiled at him. "*Pindai*!" I said. "Come in!"

He came in and shook my hand, then sat down, placing a pile of envelopes on the kitchen table. I got up to put the kettle on for tea.

"I went to the post office while I was in Masvingo, Maiguru," he said, sifting through the pile of letters. "This one is for you. It's from London."

I frowned. "From London?" I couldn't think who would be writing to me from the UK. But when I saw the writing on the envelope, and the return address at the back, I realised who it was. I started to grin as I tore open the sealed edge. "Kuziwa," I said excitedly, "this letter is from Rutendo Machingaidze, my classmate from agricultural college. She went on to study at the University of Zimbabwe - she was so clever, that one! The last I heard, she was doing a Masters and writing books, can you imagine?"

Kuziwa nodded, smiling, amused by my girlish excitement. But I remembered those days studying at the college, me, always the oldest student in the class, discussing farming practice with young people who had never held a hoe in their hands. As I came to realise, some of them never would.

After college, Rutendo and I kept in contact but only saw each other a few times. She went her way and I went mine. I heard that she married a *murungu* but I could never quite believe it – she had always seemed so cultural, so sure of her roots. I wouldn't have thought that she would ever consider marrying a non-Shona, let alone a *murungu*. But when we spoke, she told me that her husband was different from the others, that he was not a racist and could speak perfect Shona, so maybe that had made it easier for her family to accept him, even though his never had...

Rutendo's letter was as warm as I remembered her. She spoke of her husband, her two children, her studies at the university, and her scholarship to study for a PhD in the UK. I was touched when she asked me to come to the UK for her graduation, offering to pay for my ticket to come to the ceremony and ululate and throw money. And then I got to the paragraph that made my heart stop.

'As you know, sisi, Mukoma James has not been in contact with his family for many years. But, last year, they lost their farm and came to live in the UK. The mother left them and the father was arrested and the eldest, Katie, contacted James and asked for our help. How could we refuse? So they are staying here now, she and her twin brother and sister. I tell you, I never thought I would see the day when the children of Ian Watson of Baobab Ranch would eat in my kitchen!'

Ian.

Ian Watson. The Deputy Commissioner.

Baobab Ranch. The name on the rusted sign outside our farm, the one we had just taken down the other day when we cut down the grass and replaced the gate.

My mind reeled as the pieces began to fall into place.

"Sisi Tariro! Are you OK?" I heard Kuziwa's voice from far away and felt his hands on me, steadying me, guiding me towards a chair.

I felt a tightening in my chest, a squeezing that made it hard for me to breathe. Deputy Commissioner Ian Watson, the man who had stolen Nhamo's eyesight and changed his life forever, the man who had driven us from our land, ordered the torching of our fields and the killing of our cattle, the man who had robbed me of my innocence in the cruellest way. This man, Tawona's father, was the settler who had farmed and grown rich off our land for all those years! The irony, the injustice was too much. The bile rose in my throat.

"Tariro? Tariro!" Nhamo's voice was edged with panic as he tried to hold my shaking body, tried to stop me from retching.

They carried me to my room and Nhamo put me to bed, drawing the curtains. All the while, he whispered, "*Moyo wangu*, what is it? Tell me. Please tell me..."

But I could say nothing until at last I whispered, "Nhamo, please, leave me. I must have time to think... please."

And he left me there in the dark, wrapped in a red blanket. And I was able to think, really think about all that had happened and what was yet to come.

It occurred to me that, ever since the year I turned fourteen, when so many terrible things happened to me and to those I loved, I had decided to be strong. From being stripped of our land and moving to the reserve to losing Amai and my baby sister, from being raped by Deputy Commissioner Ian Watson to Tawona's birth, from learning to read to leaving to fight in the bush, I had learned to rise above my circumstances, to look things in the eye and never back down, to be brave and determined, always.

Now, when the time came to face the man who had forced his way into my life and my family's history, I could not bear it. For I knew, somewhere in my bones, that if I went to Rutendo's home in London, I would see him again. And I could not find the strength, not now that things were looking up for us, not now that we were settling into a new life.

I could not bear the thought of seeing him again, of hearing his voice, of looking into those blue, blue eyes, so much like my daughter's, of dragging up all those old memories, nightmares of *sjamboks* and bleeding skin and burning thatch and wanting to be swallowed up by the earth and never, never seeing the light of day again. And what of meeting his other children, Tawona's brother and sisters? And meeting his brother, Rutendo's husband?

I couldn't do it. All of a sudden, I felt too old, too old and too tired. Everything that I had worked for was about to come to fruition. I was not going to let Ian Watson take it away from me, not this time. Not again.

In the end, it was Nhamo who convinced me to go. He called Tawona, and she left her family in town and took the bus to our place. Kuziwa went to pick her up from the bus stop and brought her to me.

When I saw her standing in my room, her blue eyes full of concern for me, I started to cry again.

"Hush, Amai," she said gently, holding me. "You mustn't cry. You must be strong, especially now."

"What did Baba tell you?"

"He told me about the letter, Amai. He told me what happened when you read it. He knows."

"He knows? What do you mean? What does he know?" I felt a familiar panic rising in my chest at the thought of Nhamo, my beloved, finding out my darkest secret.

"He knows everything, Amai."

"Everything?"

"Everything."

I was silenced, trying to blink back tears, my hand to my mouth. What I had feared most had come to pass.

I heard his familiar footsteps at the door and I turned away, unable to look at him as he came towards the bed. He sat down and put his hand on my back, as he always did. I flinched at this familiar gesture.

"Tariro," he said quietly. "Why are you turning away? Who are you hiding from? There is no need to hide, not from me. I know what happened. And I know who Tawona's father is..."

"How long have you known, Nhamo?"

"I have always known. I heard rumours of what happened when we still lived on the reserve. And many people commented on Tawona's looks, her blue eyes. You can't hide things like that..."

"But how... why did you never say?"

"Because you never said. And because it was not important. You were not to blame for what he did, just as Tawona was not to blame for who her father was.

It did not make me love you – or Tawona – any less."

I held my breath, hardly daring to believe what I was hearing.

But he continued. "My only question, Tariro, is why did you not trust me enough to share this with me? Didn't you know me well enough to know that it would not have changed anything? Did you think I was that shallow, that unfeeling?"

I shook my head.

"I could have helped you heal, Tariro, as you could have helped me. We are bound together, you and I. Our struggles are one. Our challenges are one. If you succeed, I succeed and if I succeed, so do you. As for me, I long ago learned to forgive. Maybe not to forget, but to forgive. Even someone like Ian Watson. I have no wish to meet him ever again. It is enough that we have Tawona, that she is ours, and that we finally have the land back. That is retribution enough for me. There is no room for bitterness in my heart, only compassion and hope for the future. But you, you must go and find your peace. I know you, Tariro, you are a fighter. You must go and settle this. Your heart will never be easy if you do not."

"And I will come with you, Amai," said Tariro. "I also want to settle things. I need to see this man for myself. And he needs to see me."

So it was decided. We would go to the UK together, to confront our past together.

34
Speaking honestly

I couldn't feel excited about Rutendo's old friend's arrival. I just couldn't.

Ever since she had told me that her friend and her family were from the new generation of indigenous black farmers, my heart had burned with hate and resentment. I couldn't help thinking about the white family that had most probably lost their home, their crops, their life's work, just so that Rutendo's friend and her family could play at being farmers.

And now Rutendo's old classmate, the ex-combatant, the 'war vet', was coming to London. I felt it was too much, too much to expect me to smile and be polite to her, after what she and people like her had done to my family. So I kept a low profile and didn't say much, politely declining the offer of going to meet her at the airport.

The whole time they were gone, I nursed my

bitterness and wondered how I should behave towards this woman who was bringing all this pain back to the surface, fresh and alive.

How was I to know just how fresh that pain was to be?

A couple of hours after Rutendo had left for the airport, the house was ready. Uncle James had put away all the clean dishes that had been drying next to the kitchen sink and I had wiped down the surfaces. He had hoovered the lounge and I had rearranged the scatter cushions.

We didn't say much. I think Uncle James could sense that I was feeling uneasy and he didn't try to include me in the general excitement that the kids felt about seeing someone from home for the first time in two years.

"What's a *maiguru*?" Jessie had asked the night before, fascinated by all the Shona words her cousins knew.

"Your *maiguru* is your mum's older sister..." answered Shupi matter-of-factly.

"Who's your *maiguru*?" Gari had wanted to know.

Luke had frowned and wrinkled up his nose: "Maiguru Janie?" They had all laughed at that.

Then Jessie had stroked the woolly hair on Shupi's

brown doll. "I miss my mom," she had said quietly.

Shupi had put her hand on Jessie's arm. "She'll be back soon – you'll see." Then she'd smiled. "Can I do your hair?"

And Jessie had nodded, happy to let Shupi play one of her favourite games.

Now the kids were watching CBBC, sitting together on the carpet, looking just like cousins who had known each other forever.

When the doorbell rang, both Uncle James and I looked at each other in surprise. We weren't expecting Rutendo back for at least another hour.

"Probably someone collecting clothes for charity," he said.

I heard his footsteps going down the creaky staircase to the front door.

Heard him open the door. Heard the silence, long, drawn-out, tense.

Then Uncle James's voice reached me at the top of the stairs. "Ian… Sue? What are you doing here?"

It was Mom and Dad.

At the sound of their voices, my insides turned to water. So much pain, so much longing, so much resentment came welling up inside me that, for a moment, I couldn't speak. I could only stare as

Uncle James, his face tense, came up the stairs with my mother and father behind him.

Dad saw me first and, relief flooding his face, he immediately held out his arms to me. In a moment, he was holding me, my tears soaking his shirt. His chest heaved and shook and I knew that he was crying too. "I'm sorry, Katie," he kept saying, over and over again.

"Mom!" Luke and Jessie had come out on to the landing and, seeing Mom, they ran towards her, screaming, hugging her fiercely.

"Where were you, Mom?" squealed Jessie.

"We thought you'd never come back!" cried Luke.

Mom was too choked with tears to say anything other than 'my babies, my babies' as her children embraced her, welcoming her home. I stood back and watched, my arms around Dad. I couldn't bring myself to look her in the eye just yet. And she didn't look into mine.

After a few minutes, everyone calmed down. Mom and Dad regained their composure and noticed Uncle James's children looking shyly on.

Jessie pulled Mom towards where they were standing. "Mom, this is Shupi, and this is Gari – they're our cousins, Uncle James's kids… have you met them before?"

Mom held back, ever so slightly, a tight smile on her face. I saw her eyes dart from the children's brown skin, to their curly hair, to the African masks on the walls, and I saw her nostrils flare ever so slightly. I knew exactly what she was thinking. And, for the first time, I saw the hypocrisy in it. She didn't know anything about them and here she was judging them already! She of all people! Her attitude nauseated me and I turned away to hide the look of disgust on my face.

Dad turned to Uncle James. "Well, James, I don't know what to say, man. Thanks for looking after the kids. I don't know what we would have done if you hadn't stepped in like that..."

"Hey," said Uncle James softly, "that's what family is for, right?"

Dad nodded and coughed, clearing his throat. "You know I have never agreed with the way you have chosen to live your life and, to be honest, I still can't say that I approve but..."

"Approve?" Uncle James' eyes flashed. "What do you mean 'approve'?"

Dad looked uncomfortable and frowned, stammering, "You know what I mean, James: this life that you've chosen for yourself… who… what you've become. Of course, it's none of my business but…"

"You're damn right it's none of your business!" Uncle James's face was red now and he turned to the children. "Kids, can you go back and watch TV? I'll be there now-now…"

The children all turned to troop back to the living room, Shupi and Gari glancing back at Mom and Dad, confusion clear on their faces.

Then Jessie looked at Mom and Dad and said softly, "Don't be angry at Uncle James, please? He was nice to us while you were away. And Shupi and Gari are our friends now... please don't be angry with them." With that, she turned and left the room.

"Look," said Mom at last, her face pinched with discomfort, "I don't think now is the time or the place, all right? Let's just take the kids and go."

Uncle James laughed softly. "You're not going to apologise, are you? You guys are really something…"

"Now look, James," began Dad, "I didn't mean it like that… it's just that you know how I feel, how we have always felt about… you know…"

"About *kaffirs*? About *munts*?"

I gasped. I hadn't heard those words in so long. They shocked me with their bluntness – and only then did I realise just how much I had changed.

"Yes, James, that is it!" Mom cried, her voice shrill. "And you, you choosing to marry a black woman – and have children with her – it's like a slap in the face to your parents, to your own people! It's just not right, it never has been and it never will be. It's a disgrace – and I'm sorry if I'm the only one here still honest and brave enough to say it!"

Something inside me shifted then. Honest? Brave? Was that what we were for judging Uncle James, for condemning him because he was married to a black woman, because his children spoke Shona? What else had he ever done to earn our scorn?

My mind raced, going back, remembering all the black people who had served and protected me all my life, who had left their own families to care for mine, who had befriended me, whom I had taken for granted and, ultimately, betrayed. I, like my family, had called them 'munts', 'darkies', 'kaffirs'. But they had names, all of them: Patience, Grace, Rudo, Rutendo, even Lovemore, the tireless garden boy.

I had never been honest.

I had never been brave.

If I had, I would have spoken up long before that day.

"Stop it, Mom!"

They all looked at me, shocked.

I took a deep breath and said, "That's our aunt, Mom, not some 'girl' you can order around. Her name's Rutendo, Auntie Rutendo. She's Uncle James's wife: a great mom, a fantastic cook – a part of our family..."

Both Mom and Dad stared at me as if they no longer knew who I was.

I couldn't bear to see the disappointment and confusion on their faces so I closed my eyes and continued. "And you know what?" Tears began to prick my eyelids. "My best friend at school was a black girl. Her name was Rudo and she had a beautiful voice, and she loved Jane Austen, and she used the same deodorant as you, Mom. But I was too scared, too spineless to introduce her to you as my friend because I knew just what you would think." I was really crying now, overwhelmed with shame. "And the gardener? The one whose name you could never remember? His name was Lovemore, Mom. His name was Lovemore..." I wept then because I smelt once again the parched, dusty air of the hot dry summers on the farm; I heard the sound of the dogs and the crickets and Rudo's voice singing, alto to my soprano. I cried, thinking of Patience, Grace, Rudo and her brother Max, knowing I would probably never see any of them again.

Uncle James put his hand on my shoulder. It felt warm and firm and I wiped my face, finally daring to look my dad in the face.

His eyes were a steely blue, uncomprehending, and he growled, "I might have known that you'd try to brainwash her, James…"

"Brainwash?" cried Uncle James. "I've done nothing of the sort, Ian! It's you who are guilty of brainwashing. Did you really think you could carry on living as if you were still in Rhodesia, living the glory days? You 'Rhodies' have brainwashed your children so that they are totally alienated from the country of their birth, totally out of touch with other Zimbabweans who do not happen to have white skin! You brought them up believing that their white skin made them superior…"

A memory stirred. 'They're not your equals. Black is black and white is white.'

"There's nothing wrong with being proud of your heritage, proud of where you come from," said Mom stiffly.

"Well, Sue, I happen to believe that we are

intelligent beings, capable of being objective, of choosing our own identity. We don't have to accept or condone everything our ancestors did..."

"I've had enough of this!" Dad growled. "If you're going to start badmouthing our parents and all those who made that country what it was, we're going. I've said my piece. Thanks again for looking after the kids but we can take it from here..."

But I didn't want to go with them then. I wanted to say that I understood what Uncle James was saying, that I agreed with him, that all I wanted was to find where I belonged, to find a way to be at peace with myself. Yet I said nothing and the moment passed; Mom asked where the kids' things were and the two of them marched off to start packing our bags.

I sat down on one of the high kitchen chairs, trying to collect my thoughts, but before I could even begin to start to untangle the emotions that twisted and turned inside me, the doorbell rang again.

And when I saw the woman who came up the stairs behind Auntie Rutendo, her head wrapped in a scarf, her smile showing the gap between her front teeth, my blood froze in my veins.

I knew her. Briefly, I searched my mind for the time, the place.

And then it came to me.

She was the woman who had accompanied the 'war vets' on that dreadful night. She was the one who had laid claim to our farm, to my home!

She was all my memories and nightmares rolled into one.

35
History

I recognised the girl, Katie, immediately and my smile faded. In my mind's eye, I could still see the look on her face as her mother fought with Comrade Zvinobaya, on the doorstep of their house, the one that was destroyed by fire. And she recognised me.

Confusion and pain flooded her face as she got up from her seat. "You..." she whispered, shaking her head. "I know you... What are you doing here? What are you doing here?" And she looked wildly around, first at Mukoma James, then at Rutendo, as if they had betrayed her.

Rutendo, always the peace-maker, gently put her arm around her and said, "This is my old friend, Katie, MaiTawona. She's come from Zimbabwe for my graduation..."

But Katie was still reeling with shock, as if the pieces of the puzzle were finally coming together in her mind, and she shook off Rutendo's arm. She started to cry. "Oh my God," she kept saying. "Oh my God."

Then Mukoma James came forward and said quietly, "My brother Ian and his wife are here too. They arrived a short while ago to collect the children."

So he was here, the man himself. My bones had not been wrong. I steeled myself for the challenge that lay ahead.

The girl, Katie, shook her head and looked at me accusingly. "I remember you. You were there that night, weren't you? You told my mom to pack our things and go. You and your comrades said you were taking back the land, that it was your land, not ours. But you were standing on the *stoep* of the house that my mom designed, the house that my dad built. That was my home – the only one I've ever had. What gave you the right to take it away from us?" She glared at me through her tears.

I was silent, trying to gather my thoughts. How could I speak to this young girl so that she would hear me, and understand my story and, perhaps, understand her own story differently?

Then I remembered what her father had named

their ranch – Baobab Ranch – and I remembered my birthplace.

Common ground.

"Do you remember the baobab tree on your farm?" I asked her. "The one that looks like it has its roots up in the air?"

She stared at me for a few moments, then nodded. "Ja, I remember it… I remember it well," she said softly, her voice choked with emotion. "I used to play there as a little girl."

"I was born at the foot of that baobab tree," I said. Her eyes widened. "My mother gave birth to me there, right there, all on her own. It's an amazing tree, isn't it?"

She nodded.

I felt a wave of tiredness wash over me and I remembered the seven hour journey I had just made. I needed to sit down, to rest my feet and to gather my energy. "Please," I said to her. "Please, sit with me."

She sat down across the table from me. Then we could look each other in the eye.

I began to speak. "Would you believe me if I told you that I know how you feel? That I know what it is to have your home stolen from you, to have your family destroyed, to find yourself in a new place that doesn't welcome you, where you cannot recognise yourself?" My heart was heavy with the memory of the dreary poverty of the reserve, the dry, sandy soil, Amai's pale face as she wasted away, the blood that flowed out of the hut that she and my baby sister died in.

She was biting her lip, looking even younger, even more vulnerable, and I thought how hard it must have been for her to adjust to this cold, unfriendly place, after the warmth and familiarity of Zimbabwe.

"What if I told you," I continued, "that it was your family that stole my home in the first place?"

"I don't believe you," she whispered. "You're just trying to justify what you did to us."

"And how will you justify what your forefathers did to us, Katie? How will you explain the fact that your people robbed us, exploited us, fought and killed us – over land that was rightfully ours?"

"The bush war…" she began.

"The war for liberation, you mean," I interrupted her. "The Chimurenga."

"Well," she said sullenly, "you won it, didn't you? Why more fighting, more bloodshed?"

"Victory is relative, Katie," I said. "It depends on what is important to you, what pushes you to fight.

I don't know whether you will ever understand the way we feel about the land, even though you yourself are attached to it. I fought in the liberation struggle, Katie. I am now an ex-combatant, a 'war vet'. Do you have any idea what that means?"

She shook her head and I began to speak, for the first time, unburdening myself to this girl who was tied to me against my will. Mukoma James and Rutendo's children and Katie's brother and sister had all come into the kitchen and were staring at me, an old woman crying tears in their kitchen. But I did not stop. This was a story they all needed to hear. I spoke of the late night *pungwes*, of the journey into Mozambique, of training with firearms, of laying landmines, of seeing comrades die, of killing, of dreaming of coming home.

"When we came back from the bush, at independence, we knew that nothing would ever be the same again. We knew that we had seen too much to ever forget, that our hands were too stained with blood to every truly be washed clean. We came back to find that our families had changed, had moved on and would never really understand what we had been through."

And I could not move the lump in my throat as

I thought of my beloved brother, Farai, killed by the Rhodesian Army; of Baba's eyes, which hardly seemed to recognise me as his daughter when I came back; of Mainini Tambudzai, forcing me to pretend that I had never been away; to forget, forget, forget. Don't speak, don't speak, don't speak of the terror, the rank smell of death, the stench of charred flesh, the hunger, the fear, the isolation. You are heroes, you must look forward, not backwards.

What's done is done.

"My uncle Ralph died fighting too," said Katie. "You weren't the only ones to believe in a cause and die fighting for it..."

"Fighting for land that was taken by force, by deceitful means? How can you justify that, Katie?"

She faltered, then said, "We were defending our way of life. There's no shame in that."

I smiled ruefully and said, "And just how did that way of life change under majority rule, Katie? Did you not keep your farms and your houses, your house girls and garden boys? And while your people continued to enjoy the fruits of the land, we ex-combatants were left to wallow in poverty in the townships, eking out a living as best we could, unable to forget all that we had sacrificed for this dream called Zimbabwe.

Some of us died in this state, our families too poor to bury us properly, our children unable to continue their schooling."

"But that wasn't our fault," she protested. "That was your black government. We always treated our black workers well..." Then her face darkened and she stopped, as if a disquieting thought had just come to her.

I continued. "Those of us who fought for independence and lived to be ignored and mistreated, we were angry. True, anger is a sin but this is the truth I tell you now: we were angry. We felt cheated, used. We did not give up our lives for abstract concepts, noble though they sounded. We did not bleed for the sake of being laid to rest at Heroes' Acre. We fought for something concrete: the land."

Katie shook her head in frustration. "The land! Always the land! Was it really that important? Was it worth everything that has happened since? Was it worth bringing the country to its knees? What have you achieved?"

"Restitution, Katie! Righting the wrongs of history! We fought for that land: the land of our forefathers. The land that was stolen from us. The land that gave us our dignity and self-respect, that made us who we were."

She was quiet then, small and lonely-looking. "So where does that leave me? Why do I have to suffer for what my father and grandfather did?"

I was suddenly overwhelmed with pity for this girl who found herself in the middle of events that were far beyond her understanding. I put my hand gently on her shoulder. "Too much anger and frustration is a terrible thing. It will spill over until it consumes all that lies in its way. I, and many others like me, condemned the violence that forced you and others like you from your homes. But you were given many chances and you refused them all. In the end, the issue of the land could not remain unresolved… don't you see that?"

"But it's just not fair," she said weakly. "We never even knew..." But then she checked herself and the blood rushed to her cheeks and she began to cry again. Maybe she was thinking of her father and his *sjambok,* his manager, Frank, who struck terror into his workers, or Lovemore, the garden boy, whose brutal beatings had brought the ex-combatants to her father's door.

I put out my hand to wipe away her tears. "You don't have to justify it, Katie," I said softly. "You just have to recognise the truth. Speak to your heart, examine it. And do not be afraid of what you find. Do not be afraid to do the right thing, even if all around you do the opposite. There is hope for you, and your brother and sister, because you are young. You can choose who you want to be. If you young people, black and white, can accept the mistakes made by your forefathers – and by us – there is hope for our country, hope for Zimbabwe."

I held her then. I felt her stiffen at first. But after a few moments, she relaxed and sobbed against my shoulder while I stroked her hair.

"Shhh," I soothed, as if she was one of my own children. "It's OK… it's OK... It will be all right…"

That was how her father, Deputy Commissioner Ian Watson, the man who was responsible for my worst nightmare and my greatest joy, found us.

And that was when Tawona, my daughter, his daughter, Katie's half-sister, came in from the car, carrying the last of the bags across her broad shoulders.

Epilogue

Tawona

He knew who I was straight away.

I saw it in his face when he looked into my eyes and saw his own blue, blue ones staring back at him.

There was turmoil: accusations, denials, tears and a lot of anger. And shame. His wife has left with the younger children. She needs time to come to terms with all that has gone before, all that she thought she knew, and all that is to come. Katie, my half-sister, has said that she wants to stay with Mukoma James for a little longer, until things settle down.

It will not be easy for my father either. I know he never thought he would see me, not here in this place, after everything that has happened to him, after what he has become.

I will give him time.

I have waited for over 40 years to face him. I have waited for over 40 years to ask him to explain his actions, to explain why his blood runs through my veins, what this means – for him and for me.

So I will wait, while they grieve, while they mourn the lies they have lived all these years.

I will wait.

And then I will take Katie, my half-sister, by the hand, by her once-sunburned, farmer's-girl hand, and tell her my story.

I will tell her about our land, about the home that was taken away because men like our father, Ian Watson, wanted to put down roots in good land and prosper.

I will tell her about the Tribal Trust Lands, the graveyards to which they transported our people and which changed forever the way our societies related to the land.

I will tell her about what happened between our father and my mother when he was Deputy District Commissioner and she was a girl of fourteen. I will tell her that he took her innocence and left her with his seed. Me.

She will struggle with that.

I am sure that is not the father she knows.

But every father is also a man, and two opposing personalities can co-exist in one person: the loving father and the racist bigot, the protector and the violator.

But I will also tell her that that was not the end of my mother's story. That she gave birth to me, a golden child with blue eyes, and raised me in the village with love and care, raised me to love and respect myself and others. She sent me to school and taught herself to read and write. She protested against the unfairness of the time in her own way. And, when the time came, she left me in the village and went to fight in the war, went to fight the Chimurenga, to set our people free.

And that was not the end of our story either.

Amai fought, as did many others, and, after much bloodshed, terror and pain, we won our freedom, freedom for everyone in our country: black, white, and even mixed like me.

Katie will not understand me when I speak of freedom. She has never experienced anything different. That is the way her life story was written. She was born free.

But she is not yet free from the shackles of history, from the prejudices and injustices of the past.

But maybe, if, one day, she returns to Zimbabwe and I take her to our home and press her farmer's-girl hand to the rough bark of the baobab at the foot of Amai's farm, she will understand. If she tastes my mother's sweet chibage and eats pumpkin with relish, picking up sadza with her fingers, she will taste how sweet freedom can be.

Because this pain, this time of turmoil in our country, Zimbabwe, is far from over. There are many more trials to come. But pain is a necessary part of life; it is part of the birthing process, part of the birth of a nation. Are not these trials like the storms in the rainy season? They wash away all the dust, clean out the debris that clogs the river. And, the next morning, the world is left sparkling with moist, fertile, new life, ready to be cultivated.

And, one day, will we not be free to plant whatever we want, to re-imagine the earth, to reap the harvest of a shared future – together?

In my heart, I believe it is so. It must be so.

It must be that, one day, no one will be exiled far from home, but all will be free to return, with open hearts and willing hands, to rebuild a home called Zimbabwe, as our ancestors built the great city of stone, Dzimba-dza-mabwe, so long ago.

Timeline of historical events in Rhodesia/Zimbabwe

1888 – Signing of the Rudd Concession by which Cecil Rhodes obtains mining rights from King Lobengula of the Ndebele people.

1896-97 – First Chimurenga (War for Liberation in Shona) - Shona and Ndebele revolt against settlers taking their land.

1923 – Southern Rhodesia becomes a self-governing British colony and more European settlers begin to arrive.

1951 – Native Land Husbandry Act is passed.

1965 – Prime Minister Ian Smith's Unilateral Declaration of Independence (UDI) from the United Kingdom.

1966-79 Second Chimurenga – Zimbabwe African National Union (ZANU) and Zimbabwe African Political Union (ZAPU) launch armed struggle against Rhodesian forces. Known as the Bush War by Rhodesians.

1979 – Constitutional talks are initiated by the British at Lancaster House.

1980 – First multi-ethnic elections held, the country gains independence and is renamed Zimbabwe. Robert Mugabe is named President.

1990s – Economic reforms lead to hyperinflation and economic hardships for ordinary Zimbabweans.

2000 – Indigenous Zimbabweans, including war veterans, begin invading white-owned farms, expelling farmers and their workers. The government launches the 'Fast-track Resettlement Programme' and dubs it the Third Chimurenga.

2000s – EU, US and other countries impose sanctions on Zimbabwe.

Acknowledgements

Bismillah

I would like to thank the following, without whom this book would not be what it is: my dedicated readers, Muchayeva Nyandoro and 'Uncle Mike' Hamilton, who replied tirelessly to my ceaseless emails. Grateful thanks to my English teacher, Norma Nyandoro-Nkomo, who pushed me to write beyond myself, Atiyya, who fell in love with Tariro, my sister, Gugu, who said the story was too sad, Perseverance, my cultural connection, Sara and Nur, who bullied me into finishing so that they could read the story, Uncle Richard and Auntie Pushpa, for the anecdotes, our Facebook group for the encouragement and support, my agent, Sheri, for being my biggest fan, and my editor Janetta, for trusting me, and all the others, too numerous to name, who helped shape this narrative.

Lastly, thanks to my father, Dr Robert 'Mshengu' McLaren, who forced me to 'squeeze the lemon to the last drop'.

Na'ima B Robert was born Thando Nomhle McLaren
and is descended from Scottish Highlanders
on her father's side and the Zulu people on her
mother's side. She was born in Leeds, and grew up
in post-independence Zimbabwe.
At high school, her loves included African history,
performing arts, public speaking and writing
stories that shocked her teachers.
She is the author of several multicultural picture
books, including *Ramadan Moon*, with Shirin Adl.
Her previous novels for teenagers include
From Somalia, with love and *Boy vs. Girl*.
Far from Home is her first book inspired
by her African roots.
Na'ima has four children and divides her time
between London and Cairo.

For reader's guides, interviews and further reading,
visit www.far-from-home.com
To find out more about Na'ima B. Robert,
visit www.naimabrobert.co.uk